Millie's
Fiery
Trial

Millie's Fiery Trial

BOOK EIGHT
of the
*A Life of Faith:
Millie Keith*
Series

Based on the characters by
Martha Finley

MCP
Mission City Press

Franklin, Tennessee

Book Eight of the *A Life of Faith: Millie Keith* Series

Millie's Fiery Trial
Copyright © 2003, Mission City Press, Inc. All Rights Reserved.

Published by Mission City Press, Inc.

This book is based on the characters of the *Mildred Keith* novels written by Martha Finley and first published in 1876 by Dodd, Mead & Company.

Adaptation Written by: Kersten Hamilton
Cover & Interior Design: Richmond & Williams
Cover Photography: Michelle Grisco Photography
Typesetting: BookSetters

For more information, write to Mission City Press at 202 Second Avenue South, Franklin, Tennessee 37064, or visit our Web Site at: **www.alifeoffaith.com.**

For a FREE catalog call 1-800-840-2641.

Library of Congress Catalog Card Number: 2003107251
Finley, Martha
        Millie's Fiery Trial
        Book Eight of the *A Life of Faith: Millie Keith* Series
        Hardcover: ISBN-10: 1-928749-16-X
                          ISBN-13: 978-1-928749-16-5
        Softcover: ISBN-10: 1-928749-48-8
                          ISBN-13: 978-1-928749-48-6

Printed in the United States of America
3 4 5 6 7 8 9 10 — 12 11 10 09 08 07

DEDICATION

This book is
dedicated to
the memory of
MARTHA FINLEY
1828—1909

Martha Finley was a woman of God
clearly committed to advancing the cause of Christ
through stories of people who sought
to reflect Christian character in everyday life.
Although written in an era very different from ours,
her works still inspire both young and old
to seek to know and follow the living God.

*I*n *Millie's Fiery Trial*, the final title in the *A Life of Faith: Millie Keith* Series, you are invited to join Millie on the foreign mission field of Bolivia. Our story resumes in the late summer of 1843, in Orofino, Bolivia. Millie, Charles, and their friend Otis Lochneer are facing the challenges of sharing Christ in a strange culture. Though Millie has served as a homeland missionary all of her life, taking Jesus to her neighbors and friends, she is about to find her own faith challenged in this foreign country.

∞ LIFE AND TIMES IN BOLIVIA ∞

If you were to travel from the United States to Bolivia, you might be amazed at the grand cathedrals and palaces that were built when Bolivia was a wealthy colony of Spain. There is even one European-style castle with stone spires pointing to the sky like needles. Even more amazing are the older ruins of the Inca Empire, a culture that probably equalled the Egyptian dynasties in power, wealth, and scientific achievement.

But the lifestyle of the Bolivian people today is sharply divided. There are many girls in the large cities, such as La Paz, Santa Cruz, and Cochabamba, who live much the way we do in the United States. But you would also see many poor people scratching out a living by farming potatoes and corn—their children sickly because of malnutrition. You would consider yourself very blessed to live in a wealthy country like the United States.

In Millie Landreth's day, however, those differences did not exist. In 1843, poor people in the United States worked sunup to sundown just to stay alive. Poor people in Bolivia did the same thing. Their clothing and language were different, but they lived and worked under the same hard conditions that Millie faced when she first moved to the frontier. The luxuries of life—fine clothing, servants to do your washing, cooking, cleaning, and sewing—were available only to the rich, whether you lived in Bolivia or the United States. However, the slaves Millie had seen in the South lived a much harsher existence than did the poor farmers or miners of Bolivia at that time. Since their war of independence from Spain in 1825, Bolivians were no longer subjects of the Spanish Crown, but free men and women.

But freedom did not mean equality. There was social segregation in Bolivia based on race even after the war for independence. The indigenous peoples—the Quechua and the Aymara—had lived under the cruel boot of conquest for hundreds of years, but they had never truly submitted to their conquerors. They refused to learn Spanish, and only grudgingly paid taxes to the crown. The middle-class merchants, shopkeepers, and artisans were almost exclusively _mestizos_, people of mixed Indian and Spanish blood. The wealthy upperclass was predominantly Spanish.

∾ HIGH ALTITUDE LIVING ∾

The air of the altiplano, which is 12,000 to 15,000 feet above sea level, has 20 to 30 percent less oxygen than sea-level air. Millie would have had time to adjust to the elevation as she traveled up by mule from La Paz, Bolivia, but she would never have been able to keep up with a native Bolivian in her hikes. The indigenous mountain peoples have a larger lung volume and extra red blood cells to supply additional oxygen, as well as enlarged capillaries in their hands and feet. This allows better blood flow to keep their extremities warm.

Living and working in the oxygen-deprived highlands can cause people to experience dizziness, headaches, fatigue, and upset stomachs. Today we call this "altitude sickness." To relieve the symptoms of altitude sickness, the local people chewed coca leaves. The leaves are very high in carbohydrates and minerals, both of which are needed to sustain the human body at high altitudes. In 1886 Dr. Stith Pemberton, a pharmacist from Columbus, Georgia, created a drink using the coca plant: Coca-Cola.

∞ CHRISTIANITY IN BOLIVIA ∞

The first missionaries to arrive in Bolivia were Catholic priests. The native people were treated cruelly by the Spanish conquistadors, and many of the Catholic missionaries petitioned the church and the crown on their behalf. Catholic missionaries produced the first portions of Scripture in both Aymara and Quechua. However, many of these same missionaries were martyred by the people they had come to teach about Christianity.

Not all church officials believed that the peasants needed the Word of God in their own language. Unfortunately, the stance of the Catholic Church at that time was that lay people—believers who had not gone to school to be a monk, nun, or priest—should not read the Bible, as it was considered too hard for them to understand and apply correctly. It was also believed that imperfectly translating the Word of God would corrupt it.

Foreword

Without the Word of God, even sincere converts to Christianity did not understand that Jesus was God. They took the teachings of the church and simply incorporated them into their own religious system. The God the Catholic priests prayed to replaced their sun god, and offerings were made to the Catholic saints instead of the mountain spirits. They worshiped Mary the mother of Jesus the same way they worshipped "Pachamama," whom they considered mother goddess of the earth.

An excellent example of this is the practice of the "Christian" miners at Potosi's Cerro Rico silver mines today. At the entrance to the mines stands an altar with a cross on it. A miner will offer tobacco, alcohol, or coca leaves to God, asking for His protection before entering the mines. A little lower in the mine is another altar, this one belonging to Satan, who is also called Tio Sopay. He has goat horns and a solid silver heart. Here the miners will pray to Satan, giving him the same offerings of tobacco, alcohol, and coca leaves. They will ask for his protection and help in finding a vein of silver. In many affluent Catholic homes in Bolivia today, when a toast is offered, the first drop of wine is poured out as an offering to Pachamama.

In a way, the Catholic priests were right. Simply handing someone a Bible, even in their own language, or asking them to accept Jesus as their Lord, is not enough. The church must live among the people of Bolivia in order for them to grow in understanding of the Good News of Jesus Christ.

❧ BIBLE AGENTS ❧

In the 1830s, Bible agents, young men from the British and Foreign Bible Society, came to South America with

backpacks full of Bibles. They would hike through the land giving Bibles to anyone who agreed to conduct a Bible study. Many Bible agents gave their lives trying to carry the Scriptures to the villages of Bolivia. The first permanent Protestant mission was not planted in Bolivia until the 1890s—well after Millie Landreth's day.

∾ A PERILOUS CALLING ∾

Missionaries in the 1800s knew they were traveling into peril. Many—especially women, who faced the rigors of childbearing—never made it home from the foreign mission field. They died serving the Lord, joining the ranks of those faithful spoken of in Hebrews 11:36–38. They were willing to lay down their health, their possessions, and their very lives that others might hear the Good News of Jesus. They believed, as did Paul the great missionary, that they would receive God's promise in the resurrection. Many of those who did come home were too sick to continue. They did, however, tell heart-wrenching stories of the lost and dying who had not yet heard of Jesus Christ. Instead of instilling a spirit of fear in their hearers, the courage of the missionaries moved many to follow the Lord with all their hearts. Several stood up to take the place of every fallen missionary. They did not go into the mission field thinking that their lives would be preserved. They went knowing that their lives could be poured out as a holy offering. They had learned to say with Paul, "For me, to live is Christ and to die is gain" (Philippians 1:21).

KEITH FAMILY TREE

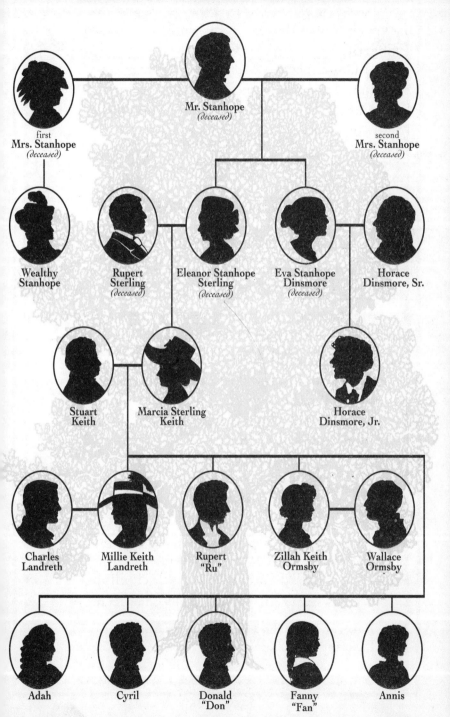

SETTING

*T*he story begins in late summer of 1843 in the town of Orofino in the South American country of Bolivia.

CHARACTERS

THE KEITH FAMILY

Stuart Keith—the father of the Keith family and a respected attorney-at-law.

Marcia Keith—the mother of the Keith family and the step-niece of Aunt Wealthy Stanhope.

The Keith children:

> **Millie**—age 22; married to Charles Landreth
> **Rupert**—age 21
> **Zillah**—age 19; married to Wallace Ormsby
> **Adah**—age 18
> **Cyril and Don**—age 17, twin boys
> **Fanny ("Fan")**—age 15
> **Annis**—age 11

FRIENDS AND FAMILY IN THE U.S.

Wealthy Stanhope—Marcia Keith's step-aunt who raised her from infancy.

Charles Landreth—age 27; Millie's husband.

Reverend Matthew and Celestia Ann Lord—a Pleasant Plains minister and his wife.

> **Joy Everlasting**—their 6-year-old daughter
> **Matthew Boone**—their 4-year-old son
> **Mary Grace**—their 5-month-old daughter

Nicholas Ransquate and his wife Damaris—friends of the Keiths.

> **Runhilda**—their 6-year-old daughter

Otis Lochneer—Charles Landreth's longtime friend.

Dr. and Mrs. Chetwood—a Pleasant Plains physician and his wife.

Gordon Lightcap and his wife Gavriel Mikolaus Lightcap—friends of the Keiths.

> **Jedidiah ("Jed") Mikolaus**—age 15, brother of Gavriel
> **Jasmine ("Jaz") Mikolaus**—age 11, sister of Gavriel

Frank Osborne—a Keith family friend.

Mrs. Prior—landlady of a Pleasant Plains hotel.

∽ BOLIVIA ∽

Don Francisco Rael—uncle to Otis Lochneer.

Angelina ("Angela") Rael—wife of Don Francisco Rael; Otis Lochneer's aunt.

Savannah Rael—Otis Lochneer's cousin, 9 years old; daughter of Angela and Francisco.

Señor Torrez—segundo (overseer) for Don Rael.

Señorita Armijo—governess to Savannah Rael.

Tomas Yupanki — a Quechua, 18 years old.

Tupac Yupanki — a Quechua, 10 years old.

Wanunu — a Quechua bruja.

Mia — an Aymara widow, age 16.

Consuela — a servant in the Rael household.

Rosarita — a servant in the Rael household.

Julio Quispe — a friend of Tupac.

Whatever the Cost

*Suppose one of you wants to build
a tower. Will he not first
sit down and estimate
the cost. . .?*

LUKE 14:28

*M*illie Landreth grimaced at her reflection. The Bolivian sun had turned her nose a shade halfway between rose and ridiculous; the sleepless night had left dark shadows under her eyes. Her white collar was smudged with ashes, and her hair, which had been pinned into a sensible French twist when she left the Hacienda de Rael the morning before, had evolved into an alarming bantam's tail.

She splashed cold water on her face and patted it dry, then she shook the remaining pins from her hair and gave it a quick brushing before she caught it up again. The wrinkled blouse and dusty skirt had to be changed, and she was late already. Millie took a shirtwaist and skirt from her wardrobe and pulled them on, taking one last look in the mirror before she left the room. *Much better. I look every bit a doctor's wife.*

"Millie!" Angela Rael reached out a hand to her as Millie entered the conservatory. "I was so worried."

It gave Millie's heart a twinge to see the concern on her friend's face. *A consumptive patient should not worry; Charles has been very adamant about that. Excess worry could cause decline, and Angela's condition is already precarious.*

"And I'm so sorry to have caused concern." Millie knelt beside the wheelchair. "Please forgive me."

"Of course you are forgiven. But where have you been? You can't imagine how I felt when I rose for breakfast and found you had not returned."

Angela stopped to cough into a lace kerchief. When she could catch her breath, she went on. "It's past noon! I couldn't eat a bite until I knew you were safe!"

Millie's Fiery Trial

"I am completely safe, and have been all night," Millie assured her. "Would you like me to push you to the garden while we talk?" The garden had a calming effect on Angela, and Charles had assured them that the fresh air full of sunshine was the best medicine for her lungs. *She certainly seems to have improved since I've been taking her out each day.*

"Yes," Angela said. "The garden would be lovely—provided you produce the whole story of your adventure. Señorita Armijo has told me that you have only just come home and that you spent the night in the village. But there is no hotel there, no proper place for a lady. And why is your nose so red? Did you forget your bonnet?"

Millie tucked a lap rug around her friend's knees, then pushed the chair through the wide doors to the garden path. Heat radiated from the adobe wall of the hacienda, warming the path beneath them. Millie parked the chair near a bench beneath a tree and sat down.

"I have been at the house of Tupac Yupanki," she said.

"My daughter's little friend?"

"Yes," Millie said, relieved that Angela knew his name. Angela's small daughter had been kept from her since she became ill. They saw each other at meals and for brief interviews, but Don Rael was convinced that the child would wear her out. "Tupac is Savannah's friend. Charles and Otis and I went there to pray for him. He has been ill."

"To pray! Charles is a doctor, not a priest. I can't imagine what you were thinking."

"Prayer is always helpful." Millie sent a silent prayer heavenward as she said it. "And it often does what medicine cannot." In the weeks they had been in the Rael home, Millie had come to suspect that Angela's faith was a matter of memorized words and rituals, not a relationship with her

Savior. But even that was more than her husband professed.

"And my nephew prayed? I don't know why Otis would believe that God would listen to him. He was never a pious boy," said Angela.

"But God did listen to him, and Tupac is well this morning," replied Millie.

"I'm glad to hear it." Angela produced a silver bell from her pocket and rang it. A servant appeared almost instantly. "Bring sandwiches and juice," she said. "I believe Mrs. Landreth may be hungry."

The woman disappeared as quickly as she had come.

"I'm glad to hear the child is well. He watches over Savannah, you know. I'm sure he would throw himself in front of a puma to save her."

"I am sure he would. In fact, the trouble he had was on Savannah's behalf."

"Are you saying that my daughter made him ill?" asked Angela.

"No," Millie said. "Do you know who Wanunu is?"

"I have heard the name," Angela's brow furrowed, "but I cannot place it."

"Wanunu is a bruja—a witch." Millie looked directly into her friend's eyes when she spoke, lest Angela think she was joking.

"You mean that old woman who mutters and mumbles around the village?" Angela tugged at her lap rug, which had started to slip off. "I'm surprised at you, Millie! To say such a thing."

"It's true," Millie said, helping her tuck in the edges.

"And if it is, what does it have to do with my daughter?" Angela asked.

"Otis had made a Sunday school of a sort," Millie said, "with the help of Savannah. Your daughter speaks Quechua quite well. They perform Bible skits for the village children."

Angela sighed. "The Lochneers have always had a gift for the dramatic. I loved Sunday school plays when I was child. I wish . . . "

"Do you remember the story of Elijah on Mount Carmel?" Millie asked.

"Oh, yes, it's quite gruesome, as I recall. The type of story the boys liked."

"A few days ago, Otis and Savannah were acting out this story to the village children. Tupac and his baby llama were there."

"Pilpintu." Angela smiled. "Don't look so surprised. I saw the children playing with the llama in the garden and asked the servants about it. But what on earth can a Bible story and a baby llama have to do with Tupac's illness? Millie, if you don't start making some sense, I am going to go mad!"

"They have everything to do with it, as you will see. Otis had just come to the point in the story where Elijah prays and God proves that He is the one true God by sending fire from Heaven. When Wanunu heard Savannah's translation, she became very angry. She started toward the child quite threateningly."

"How dare she!" Angela sat up very straight, but Millie put her hand on her friend's arm and spoke quickly.

"Tupac was on his feet before Wanunu could reach your daughter. He yelled at her, and the bruja cursed him."

"Oh, Millie," Angela relaxed back into her pillows, "surely you do not believe such things!"

6

"I am not certain I believed in them when I left the hacienda yesterday," Millie admitted. "But I assure you, I do now. Wanunu came to the dedication of the clinic we are building. She had Tupac's little llama with her. It was her intention to sacrifice the creature and bury it under the foundation of the clinic, so that the building would be dedicated to Pachamama."

"Surely Tupac did not agree! The children love Pilpintu. Savannah braids flowers into chains for her neck."

"Of course they wouldn't give up their pet," Millie agreed. "When Savannah asked where Tupac was, she was told he was sick."

"Was the sacrifice made, then?" asked Angela.

"No," Millie said. "Otis took the little creature from her, and I told her that the clinic was not to be dedicated to Pachamama, but to Jesus. Because we had defied Wanunu, the men were afraid to help us dig the foundation."

Angela dismissed this with a wave of her hand. "My husband will order the peasants to dig. They may not be slaves, but they still must be made to work. It's for their own good."

"We do not want to force them to help," Millie said quickly. "Jesus would not do that."

"Then how will the work get done?" Angela asked.

Millie held out her hand, showing the blisters she had earned the day before.

"You don't mean to say *you* used a shovel?" Angela's eyes grew large, as if such a thing were beyond her imagining.

"I do mean it," Millie said. "I would have had many more blisters, I assure you, if the most marvelous thing had not happened. It gives me chills just thinking about it."

Coughs shook Angela's frame, and Millie waited politely until they subsided.

"What was this marvelous thing?" the woman asked.

"It was not a *what*, but a *who*. A young man who came running—no, leaping—over the rocks and up the hills. It was Tomas Yupanki."

"Tupac's brother?"

"His only brother," Millie said. "He is a fine young man. He came right up and took my shovel. But the marvelous part is this. Charles had seen Tomas before, Angela. When we were in Pleasant Plains, before Otis told us of your husband's job offer. Charles had a dream, and in it a young man stood calling, 'Come help us!' Tomas was that young man! He started to dig, but Wanunu pointed a finger at him. 'You are digging your brother's grave,' she said. 'Tupac will die in the night.' "

The maid arrived with tea and sandwiches before Angela could reply. Millie thanked her, and for the next few moments Millie was occupied with setting up a tray for Angela and hoping that her stomach would not growl too loudly during her prayer of grace. Millie had eaten only a handful of parched grain since breakfast the day before. She looked up from her prayer to see Angela studying her, a worried look in her eyes.

"Surely you don't believe in this hocus-pocus, Millie?"

"I do not believe in hocus-pocus," Millie said carefully. "Tomas was afraid because after Wanunu cursed their baby sister years ago, she died of a fever in the night. And the Bible itself teaches us that we battle not against flesh and blood, but against the powers of darkness."

Angela was shaking her head ever so slightly, but Millie continued.

"After what I saw last night, I believe it. We went to Tupac's house before sunset, sending Savannah home with Señor Torrez."

"Ah!" Angela said. "She should have told me where you were, but they do not let her see me when I am agitated."

"Señor Torrez could have as well," Millie said. "He was to return with Charles's supplies. When we arrived, Tupac seemed tired and listless, but he had no fever. And then the sun went down. As it disappeared from the horizon, he collapsed in a seizure on the floor."

"Had Señor Torrez arrived with Charles's bag?" Angela asked.

"Señor Torrez never arrived." Millie did not add that she was sure the man was a follower of the bruja. "We started to pray, and—" The memory of evil rushed over Millie, and she shook her head, horribly aware of how empty her words seemed compared to the reality of the night before. Was it even possible to explain? "Wanunu worships a demon called Pachamama," Millie said. "She called on this demon, which she believes exists, and asked it to kill Tupac, as she had called upon it before and asked it to kill his sister. But through our prayers God intervened."

Angela's mouth was slightly open and her eyebrows raised. "There is a reason that ladies do not dig with shovels," she said at last, "and I believe you have discovered it. You are suffering from brain fatigue. All of the villagers offer beer and leaf to Pachamama." She spoke as if she were addressing a child. "Just as the ancient Greeks worshiped gods and goddesses. You don't suppose they were real, do you? Apollo and Athena and the rest. Surely you don't believe they sat around at banquet tables, bickering and playing tricks on mankind? Or what about the Norse gods of Valhalla? That horrid Odin! Really, Millie! No educated person would believe in such things. The people here are as simple as children, and as easily frightened."

Millie's Fiery Trial

Millie felt herself flushing. "The apostle Paul was an educated man," she said. "I believe it was he who wrote, 'The sacrifices of pagans are offered to demons, not to God, and I do not want you to be participants with demons.' And I know that Tupac hung between life and death all night while we prayed, and when the sun rose, it was over. Tupac was alive. Tomas picked him up and carried him to the clinic site. He helped us start digging again, and—" Millie felt foolish even saying it. "Wanunu came back. She was very angry, and she called on the power of her false god."

"Pachamama?" said Angela.

Millie nodded. "She said she would take what I loved most—my husband. She said she would take Charles's life."

"Now, Millie," Angela spoke softly, but firmly. "Wanunu is just a foolish old woman. Tupac is fine today; you said so yourself. And I am being very selfish. You are clearly tired and confused. You were up all night. Why don't you go to bed? I have plenty of servants to push my chair around. We'll have a nice talk about it tomorrow."

I may be tired, Millie thought as she walked to the suite of rooms the Raels had provided, *but I am not confused. And Charles and Otis are still working out in the hot sun.* She took off her boots and lay across her bed. The face of that wicked woman would not leave her mind. She opened her Bible to Ephesians 6:10. "Finally, be strong in the Lord and in his mighty power. Put on the full armor of God so that you can take your stand against the devil's schemes. . . . "

She fell asleep somewhere between the "belt of truth" and the "breastplate of righteousness."

"Awake at last, sleepyhead?" Millie asked Charles as she set the teakettle on the stovetop. It had become their custom to meet Otis in the parlor which separated their rooms before breakfast for Bible study and prayer. Although it was late summer in Bolivia, the mornings were chilly enough for a fire, and the little coal stove heated the room just enough to take the shivers out of a body. And the fire offered the comfort of a cup of hot tea. Otis had not yet made his appearance.

"Sleepyhead indeed!" Charles did not look like a man who had managed only a few hours sleep in the last two days. His slacks and jacket were immaculate, and his wayward cowlick slicked down. "I am not the one who slept through dinner last night and did not even wake to greet her poor husband."

"I'm sure I said, 'Hello, dear.'"

"You said mffffle ddddrrrrfff, and went straight back to snoring."

"I do not snore!" she said.

"That's bad news," Charles said.

"Bad news?"

"It means we are sharing our room with a grizzly bear, or perhaps a lumberjack with nocturnal sawing habits," said Charles.

"Charles Landreth!" Millie said, putting down her towel.

He wrapped his arms around her. "But you do kiss wonderfully."

Millie had no chance to reply to this with either words or kisses, as Otis chose that moment to emerge from his room, hands over his head as if he were being robbed. His shirt was not buttoned correctly, and half of the shirttail hung from his trousers.

"Otis," Charles said, "what on earth are you doing?"

"Lifting holey hands unto the Lord," Otis said, holding them out toward his friends. "See?"

They were "holey" indeed. Huge blisters had formed across both palms and then burst, leaving raw patches of flesh. "I apologize for my appearance, but I don't seem to be able to work the buttons."

Millie and Charles exchanged a look. Otis had grown up the son of a wealthy plantation owner. He had never done a true day's work until he met the Lord, and his hands were complete strangers to the handle of a shovel. Millie took his left hand. His fingers were slightly curled, and he gasped when she forced them straight, causing the damaged skin to stretch and crack along the dry edges of his wounded palms.

"Why didn't you show Charles this last night? If he had taken care of it, they would not be so stiff," said Millie.

Charles whistled sympathetically. "Didn't they trouble you in the night?"

"They did throb, but . . . well . . . I didn't think they were this bad," Otis said with a blush. "Nothing compared to Jesus' hands, I mean. He hurt His hands helping me, after all—ouch! Must you do that?"

"I must." Millie peeled away another flap of skin while Otis sucked air between his teeth. "We are going to have to wash them as well before they can be bandaged."

Otis looked pleadingly at Charles. "I thought you were the doctor here."

"I bow to greater experience when it comes to blisters," he said. "Millie will have you all set in no time."

It did take time, however, to heat the water and then clean and soften the wounds with a wet linen bandage. When she had cleaned them to her satisfaction and removed the dead skin, Millie produced a jar of ointment her Great-aunt Wealthy had insisted on sending with her. "Don't be a baby," Millie said, as Otis turned his head away and bit his lip at the first dab of salve. "I happen to know this ointment does not burn. You don't want the blisters to fester, do you?"

"I suppose not," he said. "But I'm not going to watch."

Millie rubbed the greasy mixture into the wounds, then wrapped a strip of clean linen around each palm and tied it at the back of the hand.

"It does feel better." Otis curled his fingers. "I think I could even use a shovel."

"Not today you can't," Charles slapped his friend's shoulder. "We will have to leave the construction to Tomas. We are inspecting mines with Don Rael today, and I expect to get a complete tour at last."

Charles had been to the mine sites several times, but remained above ground each time, discussing the efficiency of the operation. He was more interested in the conditions underground where the miners toiled.

"Of course," Otis said. "I can hardly inspect my father's investment from the surface. I'm going to feel a bit foolish about these bandages around the men. They work with picks and shovels twelve hours a day."

"God uses the foolish things to shame the wise," Millie said, smiling.

"If that is the case, then great things are in store for me," he said, as Charles rebuttoned his shirt for him.

"Did Charles tell you how much we accomplished yesterday?" Otis asked when he was completely buttoned and tucked. "The entire foundation is leveled and the hillside cut away where we need to build walls. My crew," he blushed when he said this, "is working on a diversion ditch so the rain will not pour down the hill into the building. I understand the rainy season here can be irksome."

"Was there no more trouble from Wanunu?" Millie asked.

"She did not reappear. The men worked much more cheerfully when she was gone. They may fear her, and I don't think anyone likes her."

I can't imagine why not. Words can barely describe what I experienced two nights ago. When I'd walked in the witches' market in La Paz, I felt as if I were walking through shadows. But two nights ago it was as if a curtain had been pulled aside to reveal another world — a world that included creatures full of hatred and evil. Powers and principalities. She shivered.

"I left your Bible by the bedside, Charles. I'll be right back!" said Otis.

Otis Lochneer had stepped onto the ship that had carried them from New York without Jesus in his heart or a Bible in his bags. He had met the Lord on that ship in the midst of a terrible storm, but a Bible had proved more difficult to find since their arrival in Bolivia. There were no Bibles, Spanish or English, available for purchase in any town they had passed. Millie had never imagined such a thing, and now sincerely wished she had filled her bags with Bibles instead of petticoats. Otis had to be content to share Charles's Bible, reading it at night when Millie and Charles could read hers together, and then returning it so that Charles could carry it with him during the day.

"Speaking of night before last," Charles said, when Otis returned, "I think the Lord gave me a verse — 1 John 3:8. 'He who does what is sinful is of the devil, because the devil has been sinning from the beginning. The reason the Son of

God appeared was to destroy the devil's work.' If what we saw was not the devil's work, I do not know what is," Charles said evenly.

"And how do we combat it? God answered our prayers for Tupac. How do we deal with Wanunu?" Millie asked.

Charles replied simply, "We keep on proclaiming the Word of God and lifting up the name of Jesus. We are not fighting Wanunu. We are wrestling with the evil powers that are working through her. We fight spiritual darkness by exalting Jesus — the light of the world."

Confidence rose in Millie's spirit. She remembered a verse and turned it into a prayer for the people of Bolivia: " 'Arise, shine; for your light has come! And the glory of the Lord is risen upon you. For behold, the darkness shall cover the earth, and deep darkness the people; but the Lord will arise over you, and His glory will be seen upon you. Lord,' " Millie prayed, "rescue the people of Bolivia who are trapped in spiritual darkness!"

"Whatever the cost," Otis added.

"Whatever the cost," Charles agreed.

A chill tiptoed down Millie's spine. *Whatever the cost.*

CHAPTER

2

Love and Cinnamon Buns

For we are to God the aroma of Christ among those who are being saved and those who are perishing.

2 CORINTHIANS 2:15

reakfast was served formally at the Hacienda de Rael, and was the only meal at which the whole household was expected to be present. Don Rael sat at the head of the table with Angela on his left and Señor Torrez, his segundo, on his right. Savannah, as richly dressed as a princess of Spain, sat at the foot of the lavish table with Señorita Armijo, her governess, who kept a sharp eye and sharper reprimand for any breach of etiquette. Charles and Millie were on one side of the table, and Otis on the other. Out of consideration for Otis and the Landreths, conversation at the table was always in English, unless Don Rael was instructing a servant.

This morning Otis was clearly the most animated at the table, describing in detail every shovelful of dirt that had been moved and the exact dimensions of the progress that had been made on the clinic's foundation. Don Rael listened politely, but Millie noted a slight furrow on Angela's pretty brow.

"I understand you had a disagreement with an old woman of the village," Don Rael said at last.

Otis turned to Charles.

"We did," Charles said. "She wished to sacrifice a llama to dedicate the clinic to Pachamama."

"You should consider this an honor," Don Rael said. "She is a very important woman in the town."

"I understand that she may have intended it as an honor," Charles said. Millie could see he was choosing his words carefully. "But I cannot work in a clinic dedicated to

Pachamama. I am a Christian, sir, and my work and my life belong to Jesus."

"There is a llama buried under the cornerstone of this hacienda," Don Rael said. "It was sacrificed by order of the first Francisco Rael."

SeñorTorrez smiled, and the wrinkle on Angela's brow grew deeper.

Lord, help Charles, Millie prayed. *Give him wisdom!*

"You hired me as a doctor," Charles said. "And I must help people to the best of my ability. Sin, sickness, and death all have the same author, and I must fight against him."

"The village needs your medicine," Señor Torrez spoke for the first time, "but not your religion. These people worship as their fathers' fathers did. There was a church in Orofino once. It has crumbled, but Pachamama's shrines have not." His words were clearly meant as a challenge.

All eyes were on Don Rael. He took a drink of mango juice, then dabbed his mustache with his handkerchief. "Otis, why are there bandages on your hands?" he asked.

"I'm afraid I'm not accustomed to using a shovel," Otis said.

"You have worked blisters into your hands with a shovel?" Don Rael looked surprised. "This is not like you, Otis. You like to dance and sing."

"I . . . er . . . I was working for Jesus," Otis blurted and blushed pink through his sunburn.

"Does Jesus make you work that hard?" asked Don Rael.

"The Bible says . . ." Otis's Adam's apple bobbed, but he met his uncle's eye, "'Whatever you do, work at it with all your heart, as working for the Lord, not for men.'"

Don Rael considered this, then nodded. "If it means they will work harder, then turn the whole town into followers of Jesus," he said, "and every peasant in the mines as well!"

Angela looked relieved, but the look Señor Torrez shot Otis was venomous.

"I am a good judge of men, and I have known my nephew for many years," said Don Rael. "Any faith that can teach Otis to work is good for productivity, and what is good for productivity is good for my mines."

"Coca leaves are good for productivity," Señor Torrez said. "They are all the miners need."

"How do we know if Dr. Landreth's prescription might not be better?" Don Rael laughed. "Like steam-powered pumps to pull the water from the mines. New ideas for a new world, my friend." He folded his napkin, placed it neatly beside his plate, and stood. "And now it is time to go see how well those ideas are working."

It was all Millie could do not to ask to be included in the party that set out on horseback. It had been so long since she had been riding, and she longed to feel the wind in her face. However, it was impossible to leave Angela alone again after the events of the last two days.

Angela suggested a walk in the garden, and Millie contented herself with the sunshine as she pushed Angela in her wheelchair down the wide paths. Angela asked to stop now and then and examine a bush or bloom.

"I hope you did not think that I had betrayed a confidence because I told my husband about . . . our talk," Angela said at last. "Anything that would disturb the peace of the village is of concern to him."

"Not at all," Millie said. "I would never ask you to keep secrets from him."

"Good." Angela looked relieved. "I know he seems hard, but he is really a very intelligent man. Wise. I would say Francisco is wise."

Millie pushed the chair in silence, not at all sure what to say to this. *Don Rael seems more harsh than kind and wise, but perhaps she sees him as Jesus intends him to be.*

"I told him everything, of course," Angela said as Millie stooped to tuck her shawl more tightly around her frail shoulders. "And I think he has a very good point. He believes your mind has been unsettled as the result of too much Bible reading."

"Too much . . . what did you say?" asked Millie.

"Bible reading." Angela enunciated her words carefully, as if she wanted to be sure she was understood. "I inquired of the servants, and they told me that you read your Bible at least once a day, and carry it with you on your walks."

Millie opened her mouth and then shut it again, completely surprised.

Angela seemed to take this as agreement, or at least willingness, to pursue the topic. "I am speaking to you as a friend." Her large eyes lifted to Millie's, and Millie could feel the sincerity in her words. "I have heard that such things—trying to understand what we cannot understand—is unsettling for the lay person's mind and better left to the clergy. They can read the Bible and tell us what it means."

"But . . . " Millie groped for a way to explain to her friend without rejecting her sincere concern. "We have no clergy in Orofino."

"That's true." Angela pursed her lips. "There was once a mission here with several monks and a priest. They even started a boarding school. I believe Francisco might have

attended it for a year. But after the revolution, the govern-
ment took the church's land and the monks went away."
Millie had seen the crumbling walls just outside the town.
"If we get another priest," said Angela, "then it will be different. Until then, we should wait."

"So . . . if there are no clergy to read the Scriptures to
you, you are better off not reading them at all?" questioned
Millie.

"Precisely." Angela seemed pleased that Millie understood her so well. "I'm sure reading about those horrible
demons in the Bible has completely unsettled your mind. It
can't mean what it seems to mean, of course. And even if it
did, if there were such things, don't you think it would be
better to let the clergy handle them? I'm sure lay people
should not even look into it."

"If the Bible were just like any other book," Millie said
slowly, "wouldn't you set your mind to study it and understand it?"

"But it isn't." Angela's brow furrowed again. "At least the
church says it's not. I come to your little service on Sunday
and I do enjoy hearing the hymns. I once even tried to read
the Bible. But I can't pretend I understood what is in it, and
parts of it were quite frightening. I can see how dwelling on
such things every day, as you do, would give you nightmares."

Lord, give me wisdom! Millie prayed. *Give me the right words
to help her understand.* "You are quite correct when you say
that the Bible is not like other books," Millie said. "That is
the very reason it is important to read it. There is no magic
in having a Bible, Angela. Carrying it with you means no
more than carrying a dictionary, or a book on vegetation. If
you don't read it and apply it to your life, it is useless."

"I prefer to let wiser heads figure out what it means," Angela said.

"Listening to those who are more mature in the Lord is important, but so is reading the Scriptures for yourself," Millie said. "Paul wrote to Timothy in his second letter that the Holy Scriptures are able to make you wise. It says that all Scripture is God-breathed and is useful for teaching, rebuking, correcting, and training in righteousness."

"I told you I have tried to read it." Angela's voice was surprisingly sharp, startling even herself. She looked around quickly to make sure no one had heard. "I have tried," she said more quietly, "and I do not understand it. I went to Sunday school as a child. I said my prayers. Everything is so different here."

For just an instant, Millie saw into her friend's heart—a flash of loneliness and confusion. "God promises in His Word that if we lack wisdom, all we have to do is pray for it and it will be given to us," Millie said.

But Angela's face had closed again, and she pressed her lips together. "In this case," Angela said, "it is clear to me that wisdom would say to stay away from the peasants and that horrible old woman. I intend to tell my daughter to keep away from her as well. Push me over there. I want to see the fountain." They walked in silence for the rest of their visit.

When Angela retired to her rooms at last, Millie slipped to her own rooms and changed into the riding skirt and sturdy walking shoes she preferred for hiking. She tied a broad-brimmed bonnet under her chin, put her Bible in her knapsack and her parasol over her arm, and started out determined to have an afternoon alone with God. She had hardly slipped out the garden door when Savannah appeared.

"May I go with you, Mrs. Landreth?" the little girl asked politely. "I have finished my lesson."

Millie hesitated. "Of course, if you run back for a bonnet. The sun will give you spots. Change into a garden dress and sturdy shoes as well," said Millie.

Savannah grimaced, but hurried to do as she was told. Millie leaned against the gate, sighing inwardly. *Lord, all I wanted was a quiet afternoon with You.* But even as she prayed, Otis's words came back to her. *Whatever the cost.* And she had to admit she did miss the girls of her Bible study—especially Jasmine, and her sisters Annis and Fan.

Fan is growing into a young lady now. You must have wonderful plans for her, Lord. She wants to know every single detail about every single thing in the world. The little girl's first sentence was, "What I want to know is . . ." Solomon in all his wisdom could not have satisfied her curiosity. Millie missed them all—her family and her friends—with a quiet ache. She had been some years in New Orleans with her Great-Aunt Wealthy before she married Charles, but somehow this was different. Even with Charles by her side, Bolivia was so much farther from home.

"I had to tell Señorita Armijo that Father said I should take more fresh air," Savannah said when she returned, "or she wouldn't have let me come. I don't think she likes you, Mrs. Landreth. She always lets me go up the hill with Tupac."

"Won't you call me 'Millie'? It would remind me of my own sisters if you did."

"I don't think she likes you, Millie." Savannah smiled a little when she said it, as if she knew her governess would not approve. "I don't think Señor Torrez likes you, either. I tried to tell Mother where you were, when Tupac was sick. Señor

Millie's Fiery Trial

Torrez would not let me. He spoke to Señorita Armijo, and she sent me straight to bed. Do you think that was right?" She turned offended eyes to Millie, but she didn't wait for an answer. "I wanted to tell Mother that Tupac was sick, and Wanunu was a bruja. Millie—" she said, stopping suddenly. "You are Tupac's friend, aren't you?"

"Of course I am," Millie said.

"Then you must be my friend too. Until you came, Tupac was my only friend."

Millie repented silently for trying to sneak away without the child. "I believe your cousin Otis is your friend," Millie said, taking the little girl's hand.

"He is my cousin," Savannah said. "He has to like me; it's practically a law." And then, shifting subjects without so much as taking a breath, she said, "I spoke to Father about Pilpintu. He said I could keep her in a pen in the garden. If I had not, Señor Torrez would have taken Pilpintu back to the village," she said. "But I knew he would, so I went to Pappa before he was out of bed. He said I could keep Pilpintu in a pen in the garden as long as I liked."

"And what will Tupac think of this?"

"Tupac always does what I tell him to," said Savannah.

"I see." Millie smiled to herself. She was sure this was true.

The climb grew steeper, and even Savannah had to save her breath, so they walked on for some time without speaking. They stopped to catch their breath at the base of a boulder field.

The sky was an icy blue—a color Millie had only seen in Pleasant Plains in winter—and the moon was a shining sliver above the mountain peak. *It's the same moon that hangs over Pleasant Plains, Lord. It's looking down on my family right now.* It was somehow a comforting thought. "Isn't it beautiful?" Millie said, pointing it out to Savannah.

"I don't like it," Savannah shuddered. "Poor moon! Tupac says a puma hunts it across the sky, eating it one bite at a time." Savannah studied the silver fingernail high above them. "It has almost eaten it all. I wouldn't like it if something ate me up one bite at a time."

"I imagine that would be uncomfortable. But maybe the moon's not being eaten at all. When I was a child, I always imagined that the moon was playing peekaboo with me. He was so large that he moved very slowly, hiding his face, then pulling his hand away again."

Savannah studied her. "You must have grown up in a very strange place," she said at last, "if you didn't even know a puma eats the moon."

"Very strange," Millie agreed, as they started walking again, following the path's winding way through the giant rocks. "The grass where I grew up is like a green carpet, covering the hills."

Savannah glanced back down the hill at the dry tufts of grass they had passed. "What would the llamas eat if they did not have ichu grass?" she asked. "They cannot eat carpet!"

"Savannah!" Millie grabbed the little girl's shoulder. "Be still!" A movement had caught her eye, a flash of color against the dry ground. It moved again—a snake, prettily banded in red, yellow, and black. The child had almost stepped on it. Millie pulled her back. The serpent lifted its head, its forked tongue darting in and out, testing the air. Millie had a fondness for the small details of creation—the mice and snakes and muskrats that God had filled the world with. *He must like them since He made them in such abundance and variety.*

Millie's Fiery Trial

"What kind of snake is it, Savannah, do you know?" asked Millie.

Savannah shook her head. "If Tupac were here, he would catch it for me," Savannah said. "And we could look it up in one of Father's books." The little girl's chin went up. "I could pick it up if I wanted to. Tupac says that there are no poisonous snakes here, and he knows everything."

Millie kept her hand on the child's shoulder. There was something about this serpent that reminded her of the water moccasins in the Kankakee marsh, rather than the harmless racer snakes that her brothers had kept in their pockets.

"Let's let the poor fellow go on his way," Millie said. "We are much larger than he is, so we will be the ones to be polite and go around."

There was a rustling, a whisper of sound. Millie looked around yet saw nothing but rocks. *Perhaps it was only the wind passing through the ichu grass.* She took Savannah's hand and led the little girl off of the trail, around a boulder and up the hill again. Millie looked back, carefully marking the place in her mind so that she would know to be cautious when they passed it on the way home. The snake had disappeared, and she could see nothing but rocks.

Millie was gasping for breath by the time they reached the top of the hill and settled on a rocky protrusion. Savannah was talking again, this time about her governess, but Millie was having a hard time focusing on the words.

"Listen," Millie said.

Savannah stopped and cocked her head to the side. "I don't hear anything. What are we listening for?"

"I am listening for Jesus," Millie said. "I come up here all alone, and I talk to Him and listen for what He will say."

"I've never heard Him say anything." Savannah looked up at the sky.

"You must talk to Him first and then listen with your heart," Millie explained.

"Oh. What do I talk about?" asked Savannah.

"Anything at all," Millie said. "He loves to hear your voice."

"I'll talk to Him here," Savannah said, choosing a comfortable rock. "You can go over there."

Millie found her own rock, warm with the afternoon sun. The Hacienda de Rael lay to the east—as substantial as a palace—its windows reflecting gold in the late afternoon sun. *Inca gold. The hope of treasure brought the Spanish conquistadors to this land. They found treasure beyond their wildest dreams, in the hearts of the mountains.*

The town of Orofino stood in sharp contrast, dead grass roofs over mud huts, windowless holes in some walls, like eye sockets, blind to the outside world. The nights in Orofino were cold, even in the summer months, and windows let the wind into the poorly heated homes, full of people who worked in the fields and in the mines. Even though Bolivia had won its freedom from Spain and there was no longer any slavery, the society still reflected the conquered and the conquerors. The Spanish people owned the land and the mines, and spoke their own language, brought from the old country. The Quechua people, who had once ruled this land, now lived as peasants.

I was here, loving the people who live on that mountain, preparing them for the day they would hear of My Son. Those were the words God had spoken to Millie on the ship, and they still echoed in her heart. When Jesus hung on the Cross, they were in His heart. He died so that they could be set free. *Tell them,* the Lord had said. *But how do I begin?* Millie wondered. *I have two languages to learn before I can tell them anything at all.* She had learned a few words in Spanish, enough to understand simple conversations. Quechua was more difficult.

Lord, I know You have been preparing them. And I suppose You must also have been preparing us. I simply don't see how we are to go about it. I wish Aunt Wealthy were here. I'm sure she would have at least a dozen excellent ideas.

The moon had climbed higher in the sky, almost overhead. *Is it looking down right now on Mamma, Adah, and Fan, watching them carry baskets of freshly baked bread or soups to their neighbors?* The thought brought tears to Millie's eyes; she missed them so.

"I think we'd best start back now," Millie said, and Savannah, who had been sitting quietly the whole time, came obediently along.

"Did Jesus say anything to you?" the little girl asked.

"He said something that He has said before," Millie replied. "That He loves the people of Bolivia very much."

"All of them?" asked Savannah.

"Yes," Millie said. "Every one. Did He say anything to you?"

"I don't think so," the little girl said. "It wasn't His turn to talk yet. I was still telling Him about my mother, and how we used to walk in the garden."

The brightly striped snake was nowhere to be seen, though Millie looked carefully on her way back past the boulder field. It must have slipped away looking for mice or lizards. Millie wished it good hunting and a warm rock to coil around as the sun went down.

Love and Cinnamon Buns

The men were arriving as Millie and Savannah reached the hacienda. A crowd of children stopped at the arching gate, peering through after Otis. Millie shook her head. He drew them like flies, wherever he went, but they were too frightened to step onto the hacienda grounds. Señorita Armijo was waiting on the porch, and Millie was sure it was Señor Torrez she had been watching for, not her employer or Savannah.

"Out rambling the hills again?" Charles said, swinging down from his saddle. Millie tried not to laugh. Charles, Otis, Señor Torrez, and even Don Rael were disguised by dust and mud, which coated them in one degree or another from their boots to their eyebrows, bringing out the wrinkles on their faces and turning their hair white.

"Are you sure you are not the one who has come down from the hill, Mr. Van Winkle? Your hair was dark when you left this morning."

Charles slapped his hat against his leg, and clouds of dust exploded from both hat and trousers. "Not down from the hill," Charles said. "*Up* from under the hill, and it has been a long journey."

"I would have caught a snake, Father," Savannah said, "but Millie wouldn't allow it."

"Madre de Dios!" Señorita Armijo rolled her eyes. "Señoritas do not catch serpents!"

"I wasn't sure if it was safe," Millie said. "I didn't recognize the variety."

"There are no poisonous snakes this high on the altiplano," said Don Rael, tossing his reins to a vaquero. "Tut-tut-tut!" He held up his hand to keep Savannah from embracing him. "Your madre does not like the mine dust on me. Imagine how much less she would like it on you! Jita, you should not worry Señorita Armijo in such a way. I do not approve of my daughter catching snakes. Is my wife resting?"

"She asked after you not half an hour ago," Señorita Armijo said.

"Tell her I will see her after I have cleaned up." Don Rael left them with a nod.

"Remind me," Charles said, slapping more dust from his trousers, "to thank the Lord that He made me a doctor, not a mining engineer. Let me help you with those, Otis."

Otis was pulling rocks from his saddlebags. He handed one to Millie, and she saw that it was marbled with thick, dark veins. "Silver," Otis said.

"It's a very nice rock," Millie said, handing it back.

"The snake was prettier," Savannah said.

"It was quite lovely, really," Millie added. "Banded with black, red, and yellow." From the corner of her eye, she saw Señor Torrez falter, and then walk on.

Charles and Otis excused themselves in order to wash up, leaving Savannah and Millie standing on the porch.

"Let's wait until Señorita Armijo is gone," Savannah whispered, "and then we can—" Her plot was doomed before it was begun, for at that moment the governess appeared at the door to collect her charge. Savannah looked back over her shoulder wistfully as she was towed away.

"Señora Landreth," Señor Torrez said as Millie started to follow them inside. "A moment, por favor."

Millie looked at him in surprise. He had never addressed her before.

"There is such a snake as you describe in Bolivia," he said. "It lives by the sea. Its bite is death. If you did see such a snake," he leaned ever so slightly toward her, "then you should be afraid. Very afraid."

"Pish-tosh," Millie said, looking him in the eye. "I have learned that if I leave snakes alone, they will leave me alone."

"And if they do not?" he asked.

"God's creatures are generally shy of people," Millie said, "and only attack when provoked or wrong-headed. I am sensible enough not to provoke a serpent."

"Maybe what you consider wrong-headed is simply serving Pachamama."

"Without a doubt," Millie said. "I met a bear once that was wrong-headed. It attacked God's children."

"What became of this loco-cabeza oso?" Señor Torrez asked with a half-smile.

"I killed it," Millie said.

His smile vanished. He looked at her for a full minute before he turned and walked away. Millie hurried to their parlor, her heart uneasy. *Was he threatening me?*

She still had not decided what to think of the encounter when Charles and Otis reappeared, minus the coating of dust.

"Father will be pleased," Otis said. "The ore samples are very good. They were not easily acquired either. I could barely get past Tio Sopay," said Otis.

"Another uncle?" Millie asked, puzzled. "I thought Don Rael was your only male relative in Bolivia."

Charles laughed. "This *tio* is no relation, I hope. The miners believe that Tio Sopay rules the underworld. The jewels, metals, and stones buried in the ground belong to him."

"There was a horrible statue of him at the entrance," Otis shuddered. "I'm sure I'm going to have nightmares."

Millie's Fiery Trial

"After spending four hours underground, I can understand why they think the place is ruled by Satan," Charles said. "It was as close to hell as I ever hope to come. The fumes and the dust were choking. We were warned to watch our lanterns constantly. If the flame turned red, then we had less than five minutes to find our way out of the pocket of gas. The men work underground for twelve hours a day, with no food but the coca leaves. They die by asphyxiation, tunnel collapses, explosions, and simply getting lost. The whole mountain is a honeycomb of tunnels." He collapsed onto a chair. "I don't know where to start."

"I was thinking the same thing," Millie said, sitting beside him. "We have been here for weeks and I have not told one person about Jesus. Not really. I knew how to go about it in the States. How do missionaries ever get started? I am beginning to feel discouraged."

"Otis seems to have had the most success in this venture," Charles said. "The children follow him everywhere, even when he has no translator or candy in his pockets."

"That's true," Millie said. "What is your secret, Otis?"

Otis flushed. "Promise you won't laugh."

"I will not laugh," Millie said.

"Will you give me a hint before I promise?" Charles asked.

"No," Otis said.

"Very well then, I promise," he said.

"I can't tell them how much God loves them, so I ask Him to make me smell like cinnamon buns." He blurted it out so quickly that Millie was not sure she had heard correctly.

"Like . . . cinnamon buns?" Charles's eyebrows raised.

Love and Cinnamon Buns

"Love must smell like cinnamon buns, don't you think? You can't walk by a kitchen where someone is cooking them, can you? They smell so good you have to go and get a taste. I asked God to fill me up with so much of His love that I smell like a spiritual cinnamon bun. I think that's why the children love to be near me. You're not laughing, are you?"

Of course love smells like cinnamon buns! Or soup and fresh bread. It smells like Keith Hill on baking days, and good things prepared for people who did not expect them or deserve them. "Otis," Millie said, "has anyone told you recently that you are brilliant?"

"Not recently," he said, blushing redder still.

CHAPTER

3

Connections and Concerns

A friend loves at all times.

PROVERBS 17:17

The sky was gray the next morning, dimmed by clouds too high and thin to bring rain, but thick enough to cast a chill. While Pleasant Plains brightened with spring, Bolivia was preparing for winter. It was too dull and cold to walk in the gardens for long, so after an hour of fresh air, Millie and Angela had retreated to the conservatory.

"It took me the longest time to grow accustomed to it," Angela sighed. "If we have snow it will be in July or August, the heart of winter here. It makes one feel positively upside down and backwards. And in the South, the leaves change with the seasons. Here there are no leaves to change, at least not apart from my garden. Will you play the piano?" Angela asked. "Play something from home, something from summertime."

Millie seated herself on the piano bench and ran her fingers lightly over the keys. *God in His mercy has always provided a piano for me, and this is one of the finest I have ever played.* It was a one-of-a-kind instrument, built in the room where it stood and made of imported wood inlayed with gold. *It's even more beautiful when you close your eyes.*

The tones were rich and mellow, the pitch perfect. Millie slipped away to this room whenever she could and played her own music softly to God—a prayer without words, offered from her heart. Almost since their arrival, she, Charles, and Otis had met here on Sunday mornings for hymns and prayers. When Millie played the grand old hymns of faith on the piano, she could almost hear voices in the chords.

Millie's Fiery Trial

This morning Millie tickled the keys, playing several lively tunes that had been popular when Angela was a belle in the South, then settling into a waltz.

Angela closed her eyes, smiling at the memories. "I want to dance again," she said when the last note had faded. "You can't imagine how I long for it. Francisco won my heart on the dance floor."

"He had traveled to Georgia?" Millie asked.

"No," said Angela, her face brighter than it had been in days. "I had traveled to my brother's home and we were invited to a ball at a neighboring plantation, Roselands. I saw Francisco standing on the dance floor, and my heart was captured."

"You can't be serious!" Millie said. "The Dinsmores of Roselands are my cousins. I spent a year with them when I was sixteen."

There was a moment of shock, then laughter, then many words and questions tumbled out as they both recalled different people and places they knew.

"It's hardly surprising," Angela said at last. "There are fewer than a hundred great plantations, less than thirty if you count only the best families. We attend one another's balls and marry into each other's families. Considering you married Charles Landreth, I should have realized that you had a connection." She studied Millie's face. "I somehow had the impression that he met you in Chicago, when he was studying medicine. Don't tell me you first set eyes on him at the ballroom of Roselands as well?"

"It was not quite that romantic, I'm afraid," Millie said. "I had traveled from my home in Pleasant Plains with my Uncle Horace. We met Aunt Isabel and the children in Philadelphia, and continued south by ship. My wardrobe was too rustic for Isabel's taste, so our first stop after the ship docked was to see her own dressmaker."

"Why, I know the very woman you mean! She made my gowns when I was in town. She's fabulous."

"She did have very good taste," Millie agreed. "We chose fabrics for the gowns, and I was selecting ribbons and trim from a closet—"

"I know the very closet!" Angela clapped her hands. "A tiny thing at the back of the shop!"

"Suddenly I was shoved inside and the door shut firmly behind me. Charles Landreth had entered the shop, and my Aunt—feeling that I was not dressed appropriately to meet the most eligible young man in town—had shoved me into the closet and locked it behind me. She said it was for my own good."

"For your own good!" Angela laughed out loud. "Of course. Isabel was always doing things for others 'for their own good,' but the good usually turned out to be her own. Let's see—her own daughters were too young to catch Charles Landreth, so she made your match, to establish family connections."

"I'm afraid I was a disappointment to my aunt. I turned down Charles's proposal that year, and did not agree to marry him until he had become a Christian and a penniless physician, years later."

"You must tell me the story." Angela settled into her pillows happily while Millie talked, stopping Millie more than once to ask questions.

"Poor Isabel," she said when Millie's story was done. "If she had known the Landreth fortune would soon be gone, she would not have been so eager for you to fall in love with Mr. Landreth." Angela smiled. "I'm afraid I foiled her plans as well. She had invited Don Francisco Rael to Roselands with the intention of marrying him to a horrid cousin of hers. Nobility in the family would have been just the feather to grace her cap, wouldn't it? But Francisco had his own plans. He swept me off my feet, and we were married before the season was over."

"Did he carry you away to Bolivia immediately as well?" asked Millie.

"We traveled the Continent for almost five years," Angela said. "Then Francisco was called home to take over the house and mines when his father died. It was five more years before Savannah arrived." She seemed to sink into her chair. "There will be no more children, I'm sure, now that I am sick. Unless I die and he marries again, there will be no son to follow in Francisco's footsteps."

"I do not think that is his wish," Millie said, laying her hand on the woman's shoulder. "Don Rael loves you. I can see it in his eyes each time he looks at you."

"He does," Angela agreed. "But not more than he loves his land and his mines," Angela whispered. "They are part of his blood. If man is made of dust, then Francisco was formed from the dust of Bolivia. It was a Rael who founded Orofino. Did you know that? Modesto Francisco Rael was the second son of a great family with nothing to inherit and nothing to lose. He became a conquistador and marched with the army that conquered this land. He won his share of gold and silver, and he was given this land by the Spanish Crown. He became richer than his brother who had stayed home. Then he returned to Spain to find a bride. He built her this house, and founded a dynasty. There has always been a son to carry on the name. Always, until now."

Millie did not know what to say, so she said nothing, but took her friend's hand and held it in silence for several moments.

"You must forgive me," Angela said at last, "for being harsh about your faith. I know it must be a comfort to you in this strange place, but I was afraid that it would offend Francisco and you would be sent away. You cannot imagine how lonely I have been. You have given me such comfort since your arrival. I would like to repay you if I can. What do you miss the most?"

"I miss my family, certainly," Millie said. "Aside from that, I miss cooking."

"Good heavens!" Angela said. "In a kitchen? Mrs. Landreth, your revelations never cease to amaze me. First it was using shovels, now it's cooking—is there anything you have not done?"

"A few things," Millie said with a laugh. "I used to bake with my mother and sometimes with my friends. Mother didn't always cook or clean, but when we moved to Pleasant Plains, it became necessary to learn. It was the frontier, after all. There were very few cooks or maids to be had."

"I suppose that's true." Angela's brow furrowed. "And one must eat. I simply do not think of ladies in kitchens. It doesn't seem to have hampered your education in music or the arts."

"It did not hamper my music, and since no amount of time or effort could have improved my art, I think it has been time well spent. I find it comforting," said Millie.

"I suppose everyone needs a diversion." Angela covered a yawn. "Your waltzes and romances have completely exhausted me. I think I am ready for my nap."

Millie's Fiery Trial

"It was more than a diversion," Millie said as she pushed the chair toward the door. "We started a Ladies Aid Society. The women of the church would cook and clean for those who were ill. I have been thinking I would truly love to start such a society here."

"I suppose you could use the kitchen," Angela said. "Though you would be a society of one."

"Oh! Thank you!" Millie said, smiling broadly.

"You are welcome," Angela replied.

After a few moments Millie said, "I've been considering what you said about reading the Bible." She helped Angela from the chair to the chaise lounge where Angela slept in the afternoon. "Parts of the Scriptures can be confusing and even frightening. But they can also bring comfort, courage, and faith. I would like to read them to you, Angela. If the two of us read together, there is no need to be afraid, and you can judge for yourself if it is unsettling my mind."

"I did hear Bible verses read when I was a child," Angela said. "My governess was a devout woman. She used to read me to sleep. I would like that."

Millie took her Bible out of her pocket, then began reading it at the first verse of Matthew chapter 1. "A record of the genealogy of Jesus Christ the son of David, the son of Abraham," she began. "Abraham was the father of Isaac . . . "

Angela had fallen asleep before Millie reached the third chapter. Millie pulled the blankets up under her friend's chin, and then tiptoed from the room.

The hacienda was very still. Señorita Armijo watched over Savannah in the schoolroom, and the servants, who seemed never to finish their polishing and dusting, moved quietly from room to room, avoiding Millie's eyes.

44

Connections and Concerns

Millie decided that since it was too cold to walk, it was a perfect day to read by a warm stove. She had yet to explore Don Rael's library, though she had wanted to since their arrival. She made her way to the library and stood in the center of the room. It was the oldest library she had ever visited, having stood for three hundred years, gathering memories and books. A ladder on rails provided access to the books on the top shelves, and Millie pushed this to the far end of the room and climbed to the top.

The books were spotless, the servants obviously taking great care to dust even the corners where cobwebs might hide. The leather of the covers was as dry as a mummy's face, but the pages inside were in perfect shape. There was none of the old book breath tainted with mildew that she had smelled in the library at Roselands or at Viamede, another Dinsmore plantation. The dry air of Bolivia was kind to books, it seemed. The titles on the top shelves were all in Spanish.

Millie climbed down the ladder, finding newer books on the lower shelves. Many of the titles contained words that were tantalizingly familiar. Finally, she found a shelf of books in English. *These must belong to Angela or Savannah.* She sighed happily over a set of novels by Charles Dickens. She took one from the shelf and started to push the ladder back across the room when a title in Spanish caught her eye. *Sudamerciano Animals.* She pulled it from the shelf. It was exactly what it seemed to be, a modern bestiary. It was less than a year old, and the penwork of the color illustrations was marvelous, comparable to any book by Audubon.

Millie sank into a leather chair with the book on her lap. In it was the puma Savannah thought stalked the moon, a cat with huge eyes and hungry fangs, sloths, birds, and snakes. Millie froze. A red, yellow, and black snake coiled around a piece of rock. *Coral Serpiente*, the caption read. Coral Snake. *Costa—that would be coast,* Millie thought, a fact that was made abundantly clear by the illustration. But the very snake in the picture could have crawled off the page and onto the path behind the hacienda. *How could it have come to be here, so far from the ocean shore?* Millie searched the page for more words that she might understand. *Toxico—does that mean toxic?* Poison? *Muerto.* This time she understood. *Death. Muerto means death.* She shivered as she replaced the book on the shelf.

Millie took the novel by Dickens back to her room and spent the rest of the afternoon absorbed in the adventures of *Nicholas Nickleby.*

CHAPTER

4

Delightful Surprises

*She watches over the affairs
of her household and does
not eat the bread
of idleness.*

PROVERBS 31:27

Delightful Surprises

It was two days before Millie found time to make her way through the labyrinth of halls to the kitchen. The kitchen itself was familiar enough, with two stoves for cooking and the smells of hams, onions, and garlic, which hung from the rafters. Aunt Wealthy had once told her that you could tell a great deal about a woman by her kitchen. This kitchen was well-ordered and neat, to say nothing of pleasantly warm.

Millie smiled at the two women who were hard at work, one rolling pastry dough on a floured board, the other peeling a pile of potatoes. The women were very similar, mother and daughter, Millie was sure, both stout and cheerful-looking with round, pleasant faces. They were clearly perplexed by her sudden appearance in their kitchen.

The older woman addressed a polite question to Millie in Spanish and offered a smile.

Millie smiled back and shook her head. "Mi nombre Millie," she said. "My name is Millie."

"Consuela," the matron said, and then pointing at the younger woman, she said, "Rosarita."

I may not speak Spanish, Millie thought as she rolled up her sleeves, *but I do speak kitchen*. There was an apron hanging on a hook, and Millie took it down and wrapped it around herself. This caused a commotion. The cooks looked at each other and spread their hands in disapproval. Millie smiled again and picked up a paring knife and one of the potatoes from the pile and started to peel it. The flesh was firm and more yellow than the potatoes Millie had peeled at home, but that was the only difference.

Millie's Fiery Trial

Rosarita narrowed her eyes, and her knife moved faster, blade flashing as potato skin flew. Millie increased her speed as well, careful to keep her fingers from the sharp blade. She finished her potato and snatched up another.

A man Millie had seen working in the garden came in the back door and stopped to watch; then he called in one of the house servants. Soon a ring of spectators stood around the table, cheering each time a potato was finished and dropped into a pile.

Millie and Rosarita reached for the last potato at the same time, but Rosarita moved faster, snatching it away. When every strip of skin was removed, she tossed it triumphantly on her pile, put down her knife, and folded her arms, and a cheer went up around the table.

Consuela waved them to silence as she examined the piles of pale, naked potatoes. Rosarita smiled as Consuela made a show of counting them. Millie's pile was clearly smaller. The smile disappeared when Consuela picked up a peeling from each pile. Millie's was thin and spiraled, showing almost no flesh at all. Rosarita's was chunky, clearly having potato left on it.

Consuela grabbed Millie's arm and raised it in victory, but with her other hand she lifted Rosarita's arm as well. Cheers erupted from the bystanders, and then clapping and laughter as Consuela presented their prize—a pile of onions to chop, along with a speech which, even though Millie did not understand it, left her laughing so hard she had to wipe away tears with her apron.

The servants drifted away, leaving Millie to watch and learn. The fire was fed, she noted, with a brown, clumpy substance scooped from a bin behind the stoves. When the onions were finished, Millie examined the bin more carefully.

Llama droppings, she realized with a shock. She could hardly keep from giggling. All of the fine food that they ate in the dining room above had been cooked here—heat provided by dung.

Millie opened the firebox, and taking a shovelful of the dung, placed it into the flames. It was very dry and seemed to burn as well as any wood Millie had used for cooking. Consuela and Rosarita nodded approval, and she fed the fire until the box was full, just as she would have done at home.

Rosarita put a large skillet on to heat, adding two spoonfuls of lard from a bucket on the shelf, and heated it until the potatoes sizzled when they were added. Millie nodded. This was just the way Marcia would have done it, frying the potatoes and onions until they were crisp around the edges, then seasoning them with a sprinkle of salt. Meat was added, and when it was done, a handful of the mixture was dropped in the center of a circle of dough. The edges folded up and pressed together to form large tarts.

"Salteña," Consuela informed her, pointing at the little pies.

"Salteña," Millie repeated. *I have never seen them on Don Rael's table. They must be for the shepherds and gardeners attached to the house.*

Consuela heaved a sigh of relief as the pans of meat pies went into the oven, brushing the sweat from her brow with her apron. The kitchen was not pleasantly warm any longer. It was quite hot with both stoves going.

The teakettle was removed from the stovetop, and Consuela poured three cups of black tea while Rosarita placed a bucket of water on the stove to heat. It was steaming by the time the teacups were empty.

Millie's Fiery Trial

The dishes were soon done, the tabletop washed clean, every bowl and knife put away, and the peelings all dumped in the slop bucket.

The back door opened and Tupac came in. Millie had not seen the little boy since he had been ill, and he was looking surprisingly well. His hair was a wild thatch peeking out from under his hat, and his grin very white against his dark skin. He had two buckets, each full to the brim with llama dung, and a cart in the yard behind him containing more of the stuff. Tupac sniffed the air as if he had followed the scent of the salteñas up from the village, just happening to bring a cart of llama dung along with him. *How he could smell anything besides that dung is a mystery to me,* Millie thought to herself with a smile.

Consuela pursed her lips and considered the dung, breaking it with her fingers to test its dryness. Tupac talked nonstop all the while. The boy was clearly bartering for the cartload of dung. Consuela frowned and held up one finger. Tupac held up three. Consuela shook her head. An agreement was finally made, and Tupac set to work emptying the buckets into the box behind the stove.

Suddenly, there was a wild squeaking sound, and Millie jumped, almost dropping the cup she was drying. Tupac laughed, picked two potato peels out of the slop bucket, and dropped them in his pocket. The squeaking stopped, and he went back for his last buckets of dung.

"There you are, Millie!" Savannah had come into the room. "I was looking everywhere for — oh!"

Tupac had pulled a creature from his pants pocket, clearly the same one that had been squeaking before, as it started again. He held it toward the girl.

"A guinea pig!" Savannah took it. The little creature had sleek red-brown fur, no tail, and little pink flaps for ears.

"Weeeek!" it cried, stretching out its neck. "Weeeeeeek!"

Tupac fished in the slop bucket for more potato peels, offering them to his princess as if they were gold. He was rewarded with a dimpled smile.

"What shall I keep it in?" Savannah asked as it gobbled the peels. "Señorita Armijo will certainly not let me keep it in my pocket."

Tupac answered in Quechua, and Savannah gave him a stern look. "You are being very rude," she said. "Millie is your friend. She can't help it if she only speaks one language."

Two, Millie thought. *But French is useless here.*

The boy flashed a look at Millie, and his smile disappeared. "A basket," he said.

"Do you speak English?" Millie asked, unable to conceal her surprise, and Tupac clearly enjoyed it.

"Of course he does." Savannah rubbed noses with the piglet. "I taught him. Some of the servants speak Spanish and some speak Quechua. But only Father, Mother, Señorita Armijo, and Señor Torrez speak English. If we don't want the servants to know what we are saying, that's what we speak. Sometimes I read storybooks to Tupac."

"I see," Millie said, still trying to recover from the shock. "I think a basket is a very good idea, Tupac."

Tupac produced a string which he tied around the little creature's middle so that it would not get away, and Savannah let it walk about the kitchen floor while Consuela paid him a copper coin and two salteñas for the dung.

Tupac ate half of one pie, chewing it carefully as if he were very hungry, and savored each morsel. When he had finished exactly half, he took off his hat, tucked the remaining salteña and the uneaten half into it, and put it back on his head. *That's certainly a unique way of carrying one's lunch,* Millie thought. *But considering what he keeps in his pockets, perhaps it's not a bad thing after all.*

"If I gave you some money, Tupac," Millie asked as he picked up his buckets to go, "could you bring me potatoes and meat from the market? And two baskets—one for salteñas and one for Weeker?"

"Why do you need a basket for salteñas?" Savannah asked.

"I'm going to make meat pies and take them to the neighbors."

"Why?" Tupac asked.

"Because I cannot speak to them yet," Millie said. "And I want them to know that Jesus loves them."

Tupac considered her solemnly for a moment, and then nodded once. "I will bring potatoes, meat, and baskets tomorrow."

Millie hurried to find her purse and gave him a few coins.

"Good-bye," Millie said as he left.

"Good-bye, friend," he replied.

"I will never underestimate the importance of correct technique in peeling potatoes again," Millie said. Charles was laughing at her description of the day's events. Millie set down the sampler she was working on. "How many Quechua children do you suppose speak English?"

"Until this very moment, I would not have thought any could," Charles said, still shaking his head in amazement.

"And what do you think the chances are of us meeting the only one who does?"

"One hundred percent," Charles said. "After all, it was his brother in my dream. You don't suppose God has been at work here, preparing the way? He knew we would need help learning the language. And that rascal Tupac kept it secret, even from Otis."

"He had promised Savannah," Millie said. "It was their secret. Today has been the most wonderful day."

"It can get more wonderful still," he said, pulling a packet of mail from his pocket.

"Not from home!" Millie said, reaching for the letters.

"Are they not?" Charles pretended to examine the letters. "I suppose you don't want to see them, then?"

"You suppose incorrectly, sir!" Millie said, taking them from his hand. "When did they arrive, and why didn't you give them to me earlier? From your aunt," she said in surprise, "and another from Fan."

"They came with a rider this morning," Charles said, "and I did not give them to you earlier because there was nothing for Otis, and I did not want to make him feel bad."

Millie opened the letter from Charles's aunt first. It was full of advice on marriage, most of it quite grim and the rest quite ridiculous, and admonitions against being influenced by native dress or customs. "Do you suppose keeping pies in your hat would catch on in Boston?" Millie asked.

"Chicago, perhaps," Charles said. "Boston is far too sensible a town. It could give new meaning to the phrase 'Keep that beneath your hat.'" Millie chuckled.

The letter ended with a promise to pray for them daily.

"She's not as bad as I once thought," Millie said.

"At least not at a distance of several thousand miles. What does Fan have to say?" Charles asked.

Millie's Fiery Trial

Millie unfolded the letter from Fan more slowly. It smelled as if her mother's lavender soap had been rubbed into the pages. Her little sister's handwriting was square and almost boyish, and the sight of it brought tears to Millie's eyes.

"Why are you crying?" Charles said in alarm. "Is it bad news?"

"No," Millie said. "I was just thinking of all the times I admonished her about her handwriting. She never improved. I never imagined such a scrawl could be so dear to me."

My dearest sister,

The desire for foreign missions is growing in me. What I want to know is, how you go about deciding where God has called you, and when. Is it possible to miss His plan, and to lead a wasted life? Horrible thought! I feel that I must be about His business, but Mamma simply refuses to think of my going this year. I am determined, however, to prepare myself. I drink my tea without honey and eat my toast without butter. Cyril tells me that I should eat bugs, but I prefer to wait on that. Have you had to face this hardship?

I am sure you have encountered deprivations and hardships of all kinds. Jaz, Annis, and I have made endless lists of the things which might have happened to you, and we make the Bible club pray about them all. Why, you might be at the bottom of the sea right now, full fathoms five, like the pappa in Shakespeare's Tempest, with pearls for eyes and coral growing on your bones. The hardest part is not knowing what you are doing.

I sincerely hope that you are happy with your wedded state, and with your doctor, but I have determined never to marry. I will be able to devote myself more fully to the Lord.

The rest of the letter contained news of Jasmine and Annis, and an uncommon amount about Jedidiah Mikolaus, who, Fan mentioned twice, had also decided never to marry, but to spend his life as an adventurer. He was planning to go west as soon as he could afford a horse.

"That sounds like a good deal of not marrying in one letter," Charles said when Millie finished. "Let's see, Fan is—"

"Fifteen," Millie said.

"And the Mikolaus boy is—"

"Fifteen," Millie said. "But that does not mean a thing."

"Of course not," Charles said with a twinkle in his eye. "Not a thing. The Keith girls were the belles of Pleasant Plains, and if I remember the young fellow, he was quite dashing. I wonder if Fan decided to become a spinster before or after she heard his plans to travel west? Of course your mother will keep a close watch on her daughter's heart, won't she?"

Millie took out a nib and ink. "*My Dearest Fan,*" she wrote. "*Stop eating only dry toast, and take a little milk in your tea.*" Millie stopped.

"Why are you staring at your paper?" Charles asked, watching her.

"I was just thinking that this is exactly how Paul must have felt when writing to Timothy," she said wistfully.

"Well, give 'Tim' my love, and tell her not to go chasing after that young man. There is plenty of time for such things when she gets older," Charles replied.

"I will tell her no such thing," Millie said.

"You will have to write your own letter if you wish to give romantic advice." Millie dipped her nib before she continued. "*Preparation for the mission field is more a matter of the heart than of the palette,"* she wrote. *"It is a matter of trusting God in all things . . . "*

Millie had filled three pages with her neat, small handwriting by the time she was done.

CHAPTER

5

Delivering the Goods

*How beautiful on the mountains
are the feet of those who
bring good news.*

ISAIAH 52:7

rue to his word, the next morning Tupac brought two huge baskets full of potatoes, onions, and goat meat to be made into pies. Millie emptied the larger basket and gave it to Savannah to serve as a house for her new pet. She then set about preparing the meat and potatoes as she had seen Consuela do the day before.

Consuela watched with interest, nodding approval when Millie cleaned up after herself while the salteñas were baking. Tupac and Savannah, who had been playing with Pilpintu in the garden, came in just as Millie was putting the last of ten pies in the basket.

"May we go with you?" Savannah asked.

"I was hoping you would," Millie said as she covered the pies with a napkin and a towel to keep them warm as long as possible. "I will need your help."

Tupac seemed very excited by the idea of giving away the salteñas. "Julio Quispe's Mamma is sick in bed," he said. "Celestina is not a good cook. Her haba beans will break your teeth."

Savannah put Weeker in his basket and fastened down the top, and then ran to get her shawl. Millie had collected a warm shawl of her own, along with her parasol and bonnet. They returned to the kitchen to find Tupac in earnest conversation with Consuela.

"She does not think poor people need pies," he explained. "She says they need beans and coca leaves to help them work."

"Ask her if her own children eat only beans and coca leaves," Millie said. Consuela shook her head no.

"The poor are God's children," Millie said. "It breaks His heart when they go to bed hungry and cold."

Consuela was not convinced, and she was still shaking her head when Millie, Tupac, and Savannah went out the door. The clouds had blown away leaving clear blue sky behind, but it was still cold. Millie pulled her shawl closer about her shoulders. *A brisk walk will take the chill out.*

Tupac trotted at her side, his bare feet visible beneath his thin, ragged pants. Tomas, his older brother, had been caring for his little brother since their father's death, earning enough to keep soul and body together by tending the sheep of a wealthier man. That and what little Tupac earned selling llama dung was their only means of livelihood.

"Tupac," Millie said, "how is it that Tomas is able to help Charles and Otis? Who is tending the sheep?"

"Señor Valencia will not let Tomas tend his sheep now," Tupac said. "He is afraid the sheep will lose their lambs in the spring, because everyone knows that Tomas has set himself against Wanunu." The boy seemed much more talkative away from the hacienda.

"What do you think?" asked Millie.

"I think we will be hungry all winter," Tupac shrugged. "But in the spring, when the lambs start to come, they will run to find Tomas. He has healing in his hands."

"Healing?" she asked.

"For the animals. If they can be saved, everyone knows that Tomas will save them. They trust his touch and his voice, and they obey him."

"Even Father calls Tomas if a horse or llama is sick," Savannah added. "May I carry the basket, Millie?"

Millie let her take the basket, though it was large enough to be awkward for her.

"It's too big for you," Tupac said, standing as tall as possible. "I will carry it."

"You will not," Savannah said. She gripped the handle with both hands, a determined look on her face.

"Why has Tomas always been set against Wanunu?" Millie asked, trying to stay close enough to catch the basket if it fell.

"Tomas says healing must always fight death. He says that Charles must have come to fight Wanunu because he is a healer. But why does he need a house to keep the healing in? Will his God Jesus live in it?"

Savannah's feet were moving more slowly, and she glanced at Millie.

"Jesus does not live in houses built by men," Millie said. "Charles needs a place where sick people can stay and be cared for—and a place to keep his medical supplies. Tupac," Millie stopped and looked at him, "Jesus is the one who fights death. He fought death for you because He loves you."

"Ouch! I have a pebble in my shoe," Savannah said, setting the basket down on the road. She took her shoe off and hopped on one foot while she shook it upside down. Tupac picked up the basket. When they started on, Millie noticed that the little girl made no attempt to take it back, but took Millie's hand instead.

"Does Jesus want me to give Him sacrifice or offerings?" Tupac asked.

"He wants you to trust His touch and His voice and obey Him, so you can be healed from a sickness called sin."

"I have no sickness," Tupac replied.

"We all have this sickness," Millie told him. "It makes us hate or hurt others, and it keeps us from coming into the presence of God."

"Wanunu is very sick with this," Tupac said.

"Indeed she is," Millie agreed.

"Tomas told me to listen and to watch. We will see who this God Jesus is. Tomas says only a foolish man makes a hasty bargain. I will ask him about this sin sickness."

They had company on the road now—men and women going to or coming from the market, leading burros or llamas with packs, others carrying the loads themselves in woven slings or strapped to their backs with leather bands. Two hundred people lived in Orofino, but three thousand lived in the hills around the village, and these carried their vegetables, grain, and wool to the market to sell or trade.

The streets of Orofino were wide dirt paths with no boardwalks between the street and the adobe mud buildings. Barefooted boys and girls played with sheep's bladder balls, a custom Millie thought peculiar, and elbowed each another as they kicked them down the dusty streets. Women were coming to and from the market in the town square.

Tupac led them straight through the market. They walked past tables covered with open sacks of beans, more varieties than Millie could count, bushel baskets of potatoes, and oca, a root that looked like a fat red sausage, as well as many other roots Millie was not familiar with. Other booths had alpaca, llama, or sheep's wool, some dyed and some in their natural colors. One booth had cheeses of many kinds, but there was very little meat. Several booths displayed statues of Pachamama, a cold-faced woman with a child on her back and snakes, toads, and turtles at her feet, and sold charms for avoiding misfortune or ill will.

They had almost passed completely through the market when a screech brought Millie to a stop. A shrunken little woman was making her way toward them. Millie didn't need to see the face which was hidden in a cowl to know who it was — Wanunu. She balanced a basket on her hip, and hobbled along with the help of a walking stick that crooked like a goat's hind leg.

The crowds parted before Wanunu, and as she passed they turned to watch. Savannah gripped Millie's hand tightly. Even Tupac edged closer to her as the woman approached.

"Hello," Millie said, trying to smile.

A rustling drew Millie's eyes to the basket. There was something living inside, she was sure. Something with scales that scraped along the dry sides of the basket. *What am I supposed to do now, Lord?* This had certainly never happened when they went to carry food to their neighbors in Pleasant Plains.

Wanunu put the basket down very deliberately, and several people backed away, but she made no move to take off the lid that hid its contents. Instead she spat to the left, then to the right, and started babbling, waving her walking stick at the sky, and then toward the mountain where they were building the clinic.

"Oteeessss," she said, and laughed as she threw the pieces to the ground, then looked defiantly at Millie, as if daring her to pick them up.

Millie struggled to think, but her mind felt suddenly foggy. Surely there was something she should say or do. Should she tell the woman about Jesus? Quote Scripture? Yes, that was it — if only she could remember the verse she wanted.

"Come on, Millie," Tupac said, taking her other hand.

"Yes," Millie said with relief. "I . . . we have important business on the other side of town." Millie did not allow

Millie's Fiery Trial

herself to look back until they reached the end of the street, but when she did, she saw Wanunu still standing alone, laughing.

"What did she say?" Millie asked at last.

Tupac pursed his lips. "She said the land belongs to Pachamama, and she will drive you out."

Suddenly they were surrounded by children, shouting, kicking, and arms flailing. They had walked right into the midst of a game. A chaos of elbows and bare feet spun around them. Millie pressed herself against the wall, holding on to the basket with one hand and Savannah with the other.

Tupac shouted and dove into the melee, emerging moments later holding a small, ragged boy by the shirttail.

"Julio," Tupac said. Julio wiped his runny nose on his dirty sleeve and smiled.

Millie smiled back, while Tupac spoke to the boy. The little fellow's eyes went to the basket and grew large. He glanced at Tupac, who nodded and smiled, then motioned Millie to follow, and started down the street again. They turned on a smaller path that led between more crowded and crumbling houses. Millie had heard someone say that adobe houses were made from mud and to mud they would return. If so, these were well on the return trip—some slumping as if they longed to be one with the ground once more. Some had cracks that Millie could see through. Sparse thatching that might have been rescued from rubbish heaps drooped from the roofs. Finally, they came to a door of ancient weathered wood in a recently mended wall.

"Millie! May I carry the basket in?" Savannah asked excitedly.

Millie gave Savannah the basket and knocked on the door, but Tupac laughed and pushed it open. Instead of finding a room beyond the door, as she expected, Millie found herself standing in a bare dirt yard. The ground was hard-packed and swept. It served as the entry for three small buildings, each only one room from the look of them. Children spilled out from one of the rooms, crying welcome to Julio.

Two pet guinea pigs escaped from the door as well, but one of the children scooped them up and put them back inside. Tupac started to speak, waving his arms as if he were giving a speech. Millie caught her name and "Jesus," but she had no idea what he had told them.

Seven children, Millie counted as they looked up at her, their dark eyes huge. *If there are no more hidden in the huts there will be enough pies.* The girls had long, dark braids and wore skirts and blouses. The boys all wore wool hats, but the two youngest had no trousers, and only wore long shirts. The oldest girl, who looked to be ten, was holding a baby of perhaps two in her arms.

Celestina, whose beans would break one's teeth, Millie thought. The girl's eyes went to Savannah. She studied Savannah's dark red wool gown with flashes of white at the sleeves and snowy lace pantalets peeking from beneath the hem. Then her eyes moved hungrily to the basket that Savannah held, and she nodded. The smaller children formed a ragged line, the littlest, a tiny girl in a smock, folded her little hands and looked up at Savannah and smiled.

Savannah took the napkin off of the basket, and Millie tried not to grimace as a dirty little hand reached in for a pie. The child took one and raced to the other side of the yard to eat it. Celestina waited until each of her brothers and sisters had a pie before she took one of her own.

"May she have one for her mamma and pappa?" Savannah asked, looking to Millie. Millie nodded. Savannah spoke to the girl in Quechua, handing her two more pies. Celestina nodded solemnly and wrapped them in her apron.

"We have one more pie," Millie said when they were on the street again. She pulled her shawl around her more tightly. The wind was blowing, and there was the hint of ice behind it. "Do you know someone else who is hungry?"

"Everyone in Orofino is hungry," Tupac said.

"Who is the hungriest, then?" asked Millie.

Tupac pursed his lips. He motioned for Millie and Savannah to follow him, and led them down an alley where the houses were even more dilapidated, if that were possible. He stopped outside a door where a thin blanket hung to keep the wind out.

"Mia!" he called. A voice answered, and Tupac pulled the blanket aside.

Millie followed him as he stepped inside. It was a single room, a fire pit against one wall, the bed and a shelf of adobe against the other. Millie thought at first that a child huddled in the corner, but realized that the haunted eyes were those of a young woman. She was beautiful, with darker skin than most of the people Millie had met in Orofino. She had huge almond eyes and hair that fell in ringlets to her waist. Millie was sure it was the first curly hair she had seen in Bolivia. Her clothing was colorful, made of lighter fabric than the Quechua dresses. She stood, and Millie could see that her apron was worn high. *The poor thing is with child!* Millie looked away from the swollen belly, not wanting to embarrass the girl.

Suddenly a familiar Scripture ran through Millie's mind. "I will give you the treasures of darkness, riches stored in secret places." *Of course, Isaiah 45:3, a promise You showed me many years ago, Lord. Now You're showing me another one of Your treasures here in Bolivia.*

Millie looked around the room. It was windowless and dark and smelled of stale smoke, probably from the wind blowing down the chimney hole. There was a thin, ragged blanket on the bed, but no mattress, ticking, or pillow of any kind. The fire pit was cold and the tin bucket beside it was empty.

The girl was looking wild-eyed from Tupac to Millie. He spread his hands and spoke to her in the same tone Millie had heard him use with Pilpintu when a sound had frightened her. He took the meat pie and held it toward her. She did not reach for it, so he laid it on her bed.

"I'll pray for you," Millie blurted, and the girl's eyes flashed to her, but still she did not move.

"She won't eat it now," Tupac said. "She had a piece of cheese today. She will save it for tomorrow. Come on." He ushered Millie and Savannah toward the door.

Millie glanced back at the shivering girl. "Wait, Tupac," she said, taking off her shawl and wrapping it around the shivering girl. "You eat that pie," she said. "There will be more. Tell her, please, Tupac."

"I cannot," Tupac said. "She does not speak Quechua or Spanish. She does not speak at all anymore."

"You gave her your shawl," Tupac said when they were back on the street, "because it breaks God Jesus' heart that she is hungry and cold?"

"Yes," Millie said. "Now I am a little cold myself, so let's hurry."

"Who is she, Tupac?" Savannah asked. "I haven't seen her before. Did you call her Mia?"

"Everybody knows about her." Tupac shrugged. "She's an Aymara from the Yungas, the valleys on the other side of the mountains. It's warm there all of the time. She came to Orofino with her husband, Romoldo. He was supposed to marry Simeona before he went away, but when he came back he had Mia with him. She was his wife. Simeona paid Wanunu to curse him, and he disappeared in the mines."

"Tio Sopay," Savannah whispered.

"Yes," Tupac agreed. "Tio Sopay took him. That was a long time ago, before Dr. Charles and Millie came. Mia still waits for him. No one can tell her where he has gone."

"But we have been here for weeks!" Millie said. "Don't the ladies of the town look after her?"

Tupac looked at her as if she were insane. "She is cursed, as Romoldo was cursed for bringing her here. They say anyone who helps her will be cursed as well."

"How does she eat?" Millie's mind was still reeling. She had seen poverty in Pleasant Plains and in New Orleans, and especially in the slave towns of the plantations, but nothing had torn her heart like this pitiful little figure, all alone in a strange town. "What does she eat? Someone must be helping her, no matter what Wanunu says."

The brothers, of course! Tomas and Tupac have little enough for themselves since Tomas lost his job, but they are the only ones in town bold enough to defy the bruja. The image of Tupac carefully eating half of a pie flashed through Millie's mind. *Did he give the other half to that poor girl? No. I'm sure he keeps only half for Tomas, giving Mia a whole pie every time he brings dung for the kitchen fire.*

Millie's teeth were chattering by the time they reached the hacienda. She gave Tupac coins to bring meat and potatoes and vegetables for soup, and then stood as close to the coal stove as possible. She was almost thawed by the time Charles and Otis arrived. At least her teeth had stopped chattering enough for her to tell them about the girl from the Yungas.

"Tupac might have mentioned the bit about the curse before he took you there," Otis said.

"Perhaps he thought he did not need to, if we have come to fight Wanunu," said Millie.

"Or perhaps it was a test," Charles said. "To see what you would do."

"I will tell you what I am going to do," Millie said. "I am going to take care of her. And if that horrid old woman wants a fight—well, she has found it!"

CHAPTER

6

A Picnic Break

Who shall separate us from the love of Christ? Shall trouble or hardship or persecution or famine or nakedness or danger or sword?

ROMANS 8:35

A Picnic Break

$\mathcal{I}$ should see her as soon as possible," Charles said when Otis left the room. "How far along is she?"

"I don't think she will give birth for several weeks. The baby is still high. And that's a good thing, because I'm not sure she would survive the birth." Millie laughed at the shocked look on Charles's face. "You forget that your blushing bride grew up on the frontier," she said. "I've been attending grunting parties since I was practically a child myself. And my mother is the second best midwife in Pleasant Plains. I have attended many births with her."

"I had forgotten," Charles said. "After all, I met you at Roselands, where such things are not even spoken of by proper young ladies."

The next morning, Angela listened with interest as Millie told the story again.

"I'm sure Francisco knew nothing of it," she said. "Have Tupac deliver dung for a fire. I will pay for it. And take a warm blanket—no, two—when you take her the soup. Her husband was lost in our mines, after all."

Millie carried a kettle of soup into town the next day, Savannah following along with the blankets and Tupac with a cart of dung. People stopped to stare as they went through the market. Millie stopped at the Quispes first, ladling a bowl of soup for each child and for the mother, who was still in bed. The older Quispe children talked non-stop to Tupac, and followed them down the road when they started toward Mia's house.

Tupac called out before they went inside. Mia was still huddled on the bed, the shawl around her shoulders. If the meat pie had not been gone, Millie would have wondered if she'd moved at all. Celestina, Julio, and several other children had followed them inside, and Millie had to shoo them out before she went to work. She served Mia a bowl of soup, setting it close enough for the girl to reach, and smiling at her while Tupac started a fire in the fire pit and then filled the bin beside the pit with dung. Savannah left the folded blankets at the foot of the bed.

Millie hung the kettle over the fire and sent Tupac and Savannah to bring a bucket of water from the well. When this was placed beside the fire as well, Millie smiled at Mia. She had watched them work without speaking or reaching for the soup, though Millie was sure she must be starving.

"There is enough soup for two days at least," Millie said, though she knew Mia could not understand. "Tomorrow is Sunday. We will come again on Monday. Will you fill her bucket with fresh water tomorrow, Tupac?" Millie asked. "And make sure she has a fire?" Tupac nodded, a slow smile spreading over his face.

~⁓~

"We have been working on the clinic for two whole weeks," Charles said to Millie, "and in celebration, I would like to invite you to dine with us — Otis and myself — at the clinic tomorrow noon."

"A Sunday picnic?" Millie said. "I would be delighted, sir. Will we be dining indoors or out?"

"Now, that would spoil the surprise. You are going to have to wait until our luncheon to find out. But I would suggest you dress warmly. And speaking of luncheon, we will need a table."

A Picnic Break

"A red-checkered blanket?" Millie asked.

"That will do quite nicely," Charles said, "if it is large enough to serve as chairs too. And as the clinic has no kitchen, I suppose we will have to bring a basket lunch."

"Eggs and cold ham, potato salad—and watermelon?" Otis looked up hopefully from the Bible on his lap.

"Now, Otis," Millie said. "You know we haven't any watermelon.

"I know it," Otis sighed. "I miss watermelon."

Angela and Savannah joined them at their church service around the piano the next morning, but Señorita Armijo was absent. Savannah explained that she had stayed in bed complaining of her head. They prayed for her, and for Mia and Julio's family as well, before ending the service.

Millie had attended church in her riding habit and hurried to collect the picnic that had been prepared for them at Angela's request. It wasn't in a basket at all, but in saddlebags, ready to put on the horse, and the groom had already taken it. Millie selected a pert hat, and tied it on securely. The brim was hardly broad enough to protect her from the sun, but it did bring out the blue in her eyes.

"You look marvelous, Mrs. Landreth," Charles said as he handed her up to the saddle. The mountain pony was eager to go, and he pranced in place while Charles and Otis mounted their horses.

Millie, eager for the trail and the wind in her face, knew exactly how he felt. She was not as eager a few moments later when she discovered that the little pony's preferred stride was a tooth-rattling trot. He refused to lengthen to a gallop, and simply would not walk. Millie decided halfway to the picnic that he certainly did not deserve the sugar lump she had put in her pocket, and regretted the one she had given him before she mounted. If Consuela had included a bottle of milk in the saddlebags, it would certainly be churned to butter by the time they arrived.

Millie forgot about the gait when they came around the shoulder of the hill. The clinic had grown as if by magic! All four walls were up with gaping spaces left for windows and a door. The roof was still open to the sky.

"Charles! It's incredible!" she cried.

"It is, isn't it? Why don't you unpack the lunch? I'll be right back," he said.

Millie started unloading her saddlebags, happy to see that Otis would have his boiled eggs. There was indeed a jar of milk. Millie opened the lid and laughed. Thick yellow gobs of butter floated on the surface.

"Look at this, Charles . . . Charles?" For a moment she could not see him, and when he came in sight he was walking slowly around the building.

"What on earth is he doing, Otis?" asked Millie.

"Just looking for dead animals," Otis said.

"Dead animals?" Millie asked, slightly alarmed.

"Oh, dear, he hasn't told you about those, has he? In fact, I think I remember him telling me not to mention it. Yes, I'm sure he did. So if you would be so kind as to forget—"

"What kind of animals?" Millie interrupted.

"Millie, I'm sure I shouldn't be telling you this," he said.

"Then I will ask Charles myself," Millie replied.

"No! Don't do that!" Otis looked uncomfortable. "Small ones, mostly. Taken to bits, and sometimes burned and left with powders and ashes and bits of . . . stuff. It causes a big stir among the workmen whenever we find them here. Charles always arrives early and clears them out."

A Picnic Break

"Ready for the grand tour?" Charles had returned. He offered his arm and Millie took it.

"I'll bring the food along." Otis threw Millie a pleading look as she and Charles walked away. When the two of them reached the doorstep, Charles scooped her into his arms.

"What are you doing?" Millie laughed.

"I've always wanted to carry you over a threshold," he said, stepping sideways through the door so that she would not bump her head. "We stepped from the wedding to a stagecoach, and from there it was hotels, ships, and the Hacienda de Rael. This is the first threshold that is really our own, Mrs. Landreth."

"Put me down and let me look around," Millie said, laughing and squirming in his arms.

"Not until you give me a kiss," Charles said playfully.

"Otis is coming!" Millie whispered, looking over her shoulder for their friend.

"Then you had better kiss me quickly!" Millie did.

"I have just had the most marvelous idea," Charles said as her toes touched the floor. "A toll door."

"And the toll for entering would be a kiss?" asked his blushing bride.

"Exactly," Charles said. "Or possibly two—"

"I've brought everything," Otis said, stepping through the doorway.

"You were saying?" Millie laughed up at her husband.

"I was saying that . . . perhaps the idea needs refinement. Let me help you with that, Otis."

A floor of flat stones was laid atop the hard-packed dirt, and the spaces between them filled with more dirt packed in place. Otis began to lay the picnic out while Charles gave

Millie the grand tour. The clinic was larger than she had imagined, with a waiting room, an operating theater, and a room with two beds for patients who needed to be tended all night.

Otis had set plates and cups on the blanket when they returned, and Millie started to help with the food.

"No, the tour is not quite done," Charles said. "I'll help Otis. You close your eyes and imagine." Millie complied. "Now over your right shoulder is a window," he said.

"What color are the curtains?" asked Millie, playing along with him.

"The color of your choice," Charles said, "as all such things will be your responsibility. And under the window a bench for patients to sit on if they have to wait. And over your other shoulder, there is a desk—where you sit, my dear, keeping the books."

Millie smiled at this. Since the patients could not pay, "keeping the books" would involve keeping track of their small stock of medical supplies.

"And on the wall behind you, shelves of medicines, cough syrups, and tinctures; in front of your nose, the entry to my operating room. Here will be the mortar, the pestle, everything I need to fill my pharmacy. A sturdy table and a couch—"

"On which to take a nap after lunch, speaking of which," Otis prompted.

"I hope you brought extra plates," Charles said. "I think we may have company."

At this, Millie opened her eyes and saw Tomas and Tupac looking in the window.

"Come in," Millie said with a smile. "I'm sure we have enough to share."

A Picnic Break

The brothers didn't bother walking around to the door; they just hopped in the window and squatted on their heels beside the blanket. Consuela had packed plenty of food — sliced ham, boiled eggs, fresh bread, and pastries for dessert. The basket was, however, short on plates and cups. Millie and Charles shared a plate and cup, Tupac and Tomas another, while Otis had his own.

Millie served the food, and Charles blessed it before they began. The milk was still cool, and lumps of butter notwithstanding, went very well with the bread. Charles and Otis discussed the work that lay ahead, fitting the door and roof, and putting in the windows. Millie was surprised when Tomas joined in, using a few English words he had clearly learned in the past weeks, and more surprised when Charles used an equal number of Quechua words.

"Building is hard labor," Charles said. "But it does give you time to talk."

When every bite of food was finished, Tupac wiped the ham grease from his plate with his last piece of bread and belched happily. Millie packed the plates and napkins back in the saddlebag. "I'll take that," Otis said, as she started to carry it outside. He had walked halfway across the floor when suddenly he tumbled head over heels. Millie gasped as he landed flat on his back, staring up at the sky.

"Charles," she said lightly, "someone left the stool in the middle of the room again."

"I see," Charles said as he pretended to remove the invisible stool. "I will be more careful in the future."

"It wasn't a stool," Otis said. "It was a cat. Didn't you see it?" He looked from Charles to Millie. "Surely you did. Not a pretend cat at all. It was spotted. Ouch!"

Millie's Fiery Trial

"I'm not surprised you are seeing spots after such a tumble," Charles said, "or even stars. But I have never heard of anyone seeing cats. I'll have to write this up for my medical journal. Are you all right?" he asked, when Otis didn't sit up.

"Perfectly," Otis squeaked, and the color drained from his face. "But would you mind if I just lie here, Charles? I think my leg is broken." Otis grimaced.

"Broken?" Charles knelt beside him. He felt along the leg, and Otis groaned. "How—" He shook his head. "Well, you certainly are not going to be riding a horse in the immediate future. I'm going to get a wagon from the hacienda, and something for the pain as well."

"That sounds good," Otis said.

Millie made Otis as comfortable as possible while they waited, using the now-empty saddlebags as a pillow and covering him with the tablecloth. It still seemed an eternity before they heard the rattle of wagon wheels. Charles had brought his bag.

"It's hurting," Otis said, when he came back in. "Rather a lot."

"I'm not surprised." Charles measured a large spoonful of laudanum and held it to his friend's lips. "Drink up. You realize that you are the clinic's first patient?" Otis drank the liquid down. "Now we will give that a moment to work, and then we will splint that leg," said Charles.

"Millie," Otis rolled his eyes toward her, "would you be so kind as to . . . leave. I haven't sworn, not a word, since I became a Christian, but I am afraid—"

"Of course," Millie said. "I will wait by the wagon."

Tomas stayed to help Charles, but Tupac followed her. Millie took a deep breath, and let it out as a prayer. The village looked so peaceful beneath them, but Millie's thoughts were troubled—she couldn't shake the memory of the frightening incident in the market the day before.

Oteees. She could still hear the old woman ranting and waving her arms. *The land belongs to Pachamama*. In her concern for Mia she had not mentioned it to Charles or Otis. Or even to Jesus. *I should have prayed. We should have prayed together.*

Tupac came to stand beside her, and Millie wondered if he were remembering the same thing. She certainly wasn't going to bring it up if he did not. There was no sense in putting such ideas in his head.

"Otis told me that sometimes the men find dead creatures when they come to work," Millie said finally. "Do you think Wanunu leaves them here?"

"Wanunu often came here to meet with other brujas," Tupac said. "This is their place." The small hairs along Millie's neck prickled.

Millie opened her mouth to reply, but Tupac had already turned away. It was just as well, because her mind was spinning. *Lord*, she prayed, *Help me understand! I certainly never faced anything like this in Pleasant Plains!*

CHAPTER

7

Times Like This

A father to the fatherless, a defender of widows, is God in his holy dwelling.

PSALM 68:5

*O*tis spent a difficult night, but he assured his friends in the morning that he only hurt when he moved. Charles helped him into a dressing gown, while Millie prepared a chair next to the stove in the parlor. He winced and grimaced as they settled him in, but his smile was soon back in place.

"You seem unsettled, Millie," he said, as he opened Charles's Bible in preparation for their study. "I hope you are not overly concerned for me. It is not the first bone I have broken. I always mend well."

"Are you accident prone?" Millie settled onto the sofa with her Bible. "I had not noticed it."

"He hasn't been especially accident prone," said Charles as he added one more scuttle of coal to the fire before he sat beside her. "Or prone to seeing spotted cats, for that matter."

"I would describe it more as 'adventure-with-Charles-gone-awry' prone," Otis winked. "He has been present for most of my disasters."

"I have not!" declared Charles.

"Really? What about the time I fell out of a tree?" said Otis. "Charles and I were in a tree house," he explained, "and there was a bit of a cigar I had borrowed —"

"You stole a whole cigar," Charles said, "from my uncle."

"Well, that's right. I shouldn't have said otherwise," grinned Otis.

Millie was certain it would take a complete rainbow of pinks to describe Otis's blushes. At one end of the scale would be Flustered Fuchsia, and at the other Blazing Guilt.

His current shade was just past fluster. Pricked Conscience, perhaps.

"But you didn't have to grab for it," insisted Otis. "The next thing I remember I was flat on my back—on the ground, mind you! And Charles was tying his kerchief around my head. To this day I have an aversion to cigars! And then there was the time—" He looked at Millie. "But that has nothing to do with yesterday, does it?" Otis said.

"Did you have a reason for asking, Millie?" Charles asked as he settled beside her.

"In fact, I did. I don't know if this has any pertinence, but . . . " She described her market meeting with Wanunu. "Tupac seemed to believe that the bruja was the cause of your accident."

Otis's brows were knit, and Charles was shaking his head.

"That's not all," Millie went on. "The snake I saw when walking with Savannah does live in Bolivia, but not here. It lives only along the coast. I believe it is her deadly poison."

"A snake could be transported," Charles said, "and kept in captivity. But invisible cats?"

"It wasn't invisible to me," Otis insisted. "It was large and spotted."

"Are you saying that you think Wanunu somehow controls these creatures, Millie? Stumble cats and striped snakes?" Charles asked.

"I'm saying she may have had something to do with it. I certainly had the feeling she carried something unpleasant in her basket," Millie responded.

"And she was talking about our clinic site?" Otis asked.

"She was claiming it for Pachamama." said Millie.

"I think that there is a great deal of hocus-pocus and mumbo-jumbo about Wanunu," said Charles.

"I agree," Millie said.

"But?" Charles sensed that she had more on her mind.

"But I can't deny that I think there is something more involved. A great deal of Wanunu is simple theatrics, I'm sure, but I believe there is some hideous thing behind the stage, directing the show." Millie's heart beat a little faster at this thought.

Rosarita arrived at that moment with a breakfast tray for Otis, and a summons to the dining hall for Millie and Charles.

"We've used up our study time," Charles said, "without so much as opening the Bible."

Otis took a deep, slow breath. "Could I possibly borrow yours today, Charles? I have some noodling to do between naps."

"What is noodling?" Millie asked as they made their way to the dining hall.

"Using his noodle," Charles said as he tapped his head. "He needs to think."

"Do you think he will be all right alone?" she asked.

"He did not seem to be off his feed," Charles took her hand, "and you can check on him before you set out for town. Otis will mend. And I believe we are making good progress, Millie."

"Yes," Millie sighed. "A few more years and I may be able to hold a conversation in Quechua."

"A conversation? I want to preach a sermon, and I can't wait years to do so," said Charles as he followed her into the dining hall.

When everyone was seated, Don Rael inquired about his nephew's condition. Charles assured him that with proper care, Otis would be on his feet again in six to ten weeks.

"It is an unfortunate accident and unfortunate timing," the Don said. "We have pumped enough water from the Esparaza to start another tunnel from the shaft. I had hoped Otis would be on hand."

"Must you go into the mine, Francisco?" Angela asked, concerned. "Other men have mines, and they let the powder monkeys take care of these things. It is dangerous!"

"You set the blasting powder yourself?" Millie asked, surprised.

Don Rael laughed. "I learned it from my father, who learned it from his. We are still conquistadors, eh, Torrez? We have conquered a land, and now we conquer the mountain. It tries to hide the ore from me, flooding the lower regions, but," he waved his fork, "I have found a way to fight back with the Lochneers' steam pumps. Today, the mountain will tremble!"

Angela was clearly upset, but Don Francisco smiled at her. "No Rael has ever died in the mines. Ah, Mrs. Landreth! Angela informs me that we have a widow in the town, an Aymara girl. What were you thinking, buying food from your pocket? My hospitality is insulted."

"I meant no insult—" Millie began.

"It is forgiven. She will only stay the winter, I am sure, before she returns to her own people. Until then, let her be fed and warmed by the Raels."

Señor Torrez opened his mouth, but Don Rael lifted his hand. "It is done," he said. "I will help her, although I am not bringing her into this house. And no one," he looked at his segundo, "tells a Rael what to do." Clearly they had discussed Mia before breakfast and were not in agreement.

"I am glad you are helping the poor," he said to Millie. "Men work harder if they know that their families will be cared for. Is there anything else she might need?" he asked.

"A teakettle," Millie said. "Two cups, a bowl, and a plate. The girl has nothing. Oh!" A pleading look had just come from the far end of the table. "And Savannah to help me carry them."

"The teakettle and cups you may have," he said with a laugh, "but not my daughter. Señorita Armijo informs me that she is behind in her lessons." Savannah's eyes dropped to her plate. "And Dr. Landreth, how is construction on the clinic proceeding?"

Millie finished her meal while Charles described the progress they had made. She was secretly amused at the way Don Rael ordered each of their days from his seat at the head of the table, giving his blessing or mild rebuke for the work each had done. King Arthur or El Cid could hardly have wielded a more royal authority, simply assuming his commands and suggestions would be carried out.

"I believe I will keep Otis company this morning," Angela said, when breakfast was done. "If you don't mind, Millie."

"Of course not," Millie said. "I'm sure he will be glad of the company. He is confined to an easy chair with his foot on a tuffet."

Millie pushed the wheelchair to the parlor, knocking on the door and announcing their approach before barging in.

"Aunt Angela!" Otis was clearly glad of the company, though he had been alone for little more than an hour. "Welcome to my parlor!" Solitude was never something Otis had practiced, and Millie could see he was not good at it.

"We can be two of a kind," Angela said, "and sulk here together."

"I am willing to sulk with you, dear Aunt, if you promise to recover with me. We could both be walking again in six weeks," he said. Angela laughed.

"If you are both comfortable, I will go to the kitchen," Millie said. They were, and it took her only a few moments to dash to the kitchen and throw the makings of a stew into a pot.

"I feel terrible leaving the work to Charles," Otis was saying when she returned.

"Tsk," Angela said. "It is not as if you broke your leg on purpose."

"Of course not. Millie, could you adjust that pillow just a bit?" He grimaced as she lifted his foot to do so. "In fact, I am still trying to figure out exactly how I did break my leg."

"It's not surprising you're still confused," his aunt said. "Dr. Landreth said at breakfast that you had a lump on the back of your head the size of a chicken's egg. You have very possibly addled your brains," she said. "I see from the book on your lap that you have acquired the Landreths' strange reading habits," Angela added.

"Would you like me to read to you?" Otis asked.

"Yes," Angela said, to Millie's surprise. "I would like that very much."

"We have read through Matthew, chapter 3," Millie said.

Otis opened the Bible and began. " 'Then Jesus was led by the Spirit into the desert to be tempted by the devil. . . .' "

Millie was sure Angela would seize on this when the chapter was done, but Angela sat looking at the wall, worrying the fringed edge of her shawl so long that Millie thought something was wrong.

"Will you read the last bit again?" Angela asked.

" 'Jesus went throughout Galilee, teaching in their synagogues, preaching the good news of the kingdom, and healing every disease and sickness among the people,' " Otis read. " 'News about him spread all over Syria, and people brought to him all who were ill with various diseases, those suffering severe pain, the demon-possessed, those having seizures, and the paralyzed, and he healed them.' "

" 'And he healed them,' " Angela whispered. The shawl was practically unraveling in her fingers.

"Would you like us to pray for you?" Millie asked.

"No," Angela rubbed her hand across her eyes. "I have changed my mind. I wish to be pushed in the garden. I am sorry, Otis, but it is far too stuffy in here."

Millie spent the rest of the morning with Angela, who did not seem inclined to talk, as she answered every question with a single syllable.

"I'm tired now," she said at last. So Millie wheeled her to her room.

Millie found Otis in profound noodlelation, taking notes on a lap desk as he flipped back and forth through the Scriptures.

"On your way to town, then?" Otis asked when he looked up.

"Yes, and I'm sorry to leave you here all alone, with nothing to do."

"Hardly alone," Otis said. "And I have plenty to do. I may not be able to cut a jig, but I can certainly study and pray."

When Millie entered the kitchen, Tupac was waiting for her. Consuela started up from her stool, a worried expression on her face. She took a necklace from her throat and held it out to Millie.

"Take it, Millie," Tupac said. "I told her about Wanunu. It will keep you safe."

"No," Millie said, shaking her head. "Gracias, Consuela, but no. I do not need a charm. Jesus will keep me safe. Even if He does not, I will trust Him."

Consuela put her necklace back on, shaking her head.

"Do Otis's legs belong to Jesus?" Tupac asked.

"Yes," Millie said, "they do." *Of course they belong to You, Jesus. And I still do not understand. Give me wisdom, Lord. I need some answers!* "Are you going with me to deliver the soup today?" Millie asked. "I'm afraid Savannah cannot come, but I will tell you a story on the way, the story of three boys and a furnace."

"I will go," Tupac said.

Millie collected cold meat and cheese as well as a teakettle and dishes. These last were tied into a bundle for Millie to carry while Tupac carried the soup.

On the way, Millie told Tupac the story of Shadrach, Meshach, and Abednego. "You see," she said, when the story was done, "the young men knew that God could save them, but even if He chose not to, they would not bow a knee to an idol."

Tupac considered this.

"What do you think?" Millie asked at last.

"I think," Tupac said, "that Otis tells better stories."

When they arrived at the Quispe home, instead of a line of grubby ragamuffins, Millie was surprised by happy children with washed faces and clean clothing.

"Julio's mother is better," Tupac grinned. "I told her you were coming. She has prepared a meal for you, to thank you for caring for her children."

A woman with a huge smile welcomed them in. "Chaska," she said, pressing her hands to her ample bosom.

"Tell her she does not have to do this," Millie said.

"Friends share food, Millie." Tupac frowned. "She wants to be your friend."

"In that case," Millie said, "I would be delighted. But the children must eat some of this soup." The children grabbed Millie's hands and pulled her toward one of the small structures. They pushed her inside, and Millie realized that the whole room was a kitchen. There was a chopping block, and a bag of potatoes and another of beans.

"Something smells very good," Millie said. "Oh, my!" She picked up her skirts and laughed as several of the children's guinea pigs raced past, looking for leaves or peelings on the floor. Millie was careful not to step on the little creatures as Celestina pulled her to a seat.

Chaska brought flat fried bread, hot and salty, and a bowl of beans, while Celestina ladled up some of Millie's soup for each child. Everyone gathered around to watch as Millie took a bite.

"Very good!" she said smiling.

Tupac translated, and Chaska clapped her hands and practically danced toward the fire pit, while the children went to their bowls.

"Now you will have something very, very good," Tupac said, licking his lips. "Better than salteñas. She has prepared kita quwi for us!"

Chaska turned, holding two spits she had pulled from the dung fire.

Whatever small creature had been spitted on the skewer to roast still had little legs sticking out to each side, as if it had been flattened.

Millie's Fiery Trial

Squirrels? Millie thought. But she had seen no squirrels in Orofino.

Suddenly the guinea pigs in the corner made a horrible racket, then there was silence. Millie's stomach lurched. "Tupac, does kita quwi mean guinea pig?"

"Yes." Tupac beamed as Chaska handed him one of the creatures on a stick. Millie's stomach did a complete somersault. Its little head was still attached. "Taste it!" Tupac urged as he took a bite, tearing away a bit of meat with his teeth.

Lord, help me, Millie prayed, smiling as she accepted the skewer. *Help me not to offend a woman You died for, just for the sake of food!* She lifted the skewer to her lips. "It's delicious," she said, as soon as she could swallow.

Tupac translated, and Chaska beamed.

Millie took another bite. *I ate chicken all of the time at home*, she thought. *This isn't so different. Didn't Fan have a pet chicken once? She taught the hen tricks, but that never made me lose my appetite for chicken potpie.* She managed to swallow and took another bite. It did taste a little like chicken. Chaska offered a cup of dark liquid and after the first sip, Millie was relieved to recognize black tea, very strong and very sweet. She needed two cups to wash down the last of the kita quwi.

"It was all wonderful," Millie said, "but I still must take the rest of the soup to Mia."

The children ran after her, laughing and shouting, until Chaska called them home.

"Now," Tupac said, patting his belly. "Now you are glad you came to Bolivia!"

"And I am thankful for new friends, as well," Millie said.

"Good. Tomas told me to come to him after the feast. Can you find Mia's house?"

"Yes," Millie said. "It is only a few streets away."

"And can you carry the kettle and the bundle?" he asked.

"I am fine. You do as you were told." He nodded and started away.

"Tupac!" Millie called after him. He turned. "Thank you for the surprise party." The boy smiled and went on about his way.

Millie carried the bundle over her shoulder and the kettle in one hand as she walked through the streets. People smiled at her, and some waved. *Perhaps Charles is right. Perhaps we are making progress. Or perhaps I look as green as I feel after that feast.*

"Mia?" she called at the door to the small house. There was no answer, so she stepped inside. Mia was sitting on the bed, but Millie was sure she had moved. Her hair was combed, the blankets lay neatly over the bed of straw, the floor had been swept, and the kettle Millie had left two days before was empty and scoured clean. The low fire burning in the fire pit was just enough to take the frost out of the air.

"I've brought you a teapot," Millie said, opening the bundle. "There's nothing to chase out the chill like a cup of tea." She filled the pot from the bucket of water, and hung it over the fire to heat. "I moved to a new place when I was a young girl," Millie said, just to fill the room with the sound of a human voice. "We moved from Lansdale, Ohio, to Pleasant Plains, Indiana. It was very strange to me, as I imagine it is strange for you here. I found things that I had thought were only made-up tales to be perfectly true. For instance, my brothers had a book about a mountain man, Solomon Tule I believe his name was, who lived high on a mountain and drank his coffee boiling from the pot. He had the most incredible adventures, and I was sure most of them were made up. Imagine my surprise when I found that water boils at a lower temperature high in the mountains. I don't suppose anyone in Orofino has ever had a truly boiling cup of tea." Millie sighed. "I miss it."

She set a cup in front of Mia. "Do you miss the Yungas?"

Mia looked up at the familiar word, meeting Millie's eyes for the first time.

"Do you have a family there that is missing you?" The almond eyes lowered again. "Never mind," Millie said, pouring herself a cup as well. "You have friends now, Tomas and Tupac . . . Romoldo?"

The girl's face crumpled.

Millie moved quickly to her side and put her arms around her. Mia leaned her head onto Millie's shoulder. The sobs started quietly, but soon they shook her small body. Millie held her until they stopped, and then dipped her handkerchief in the water bucket and gently washed Mia's face.

"There now," Millie began, but Mia was crying again. Millie wrapped her arms around the girl once more. "God made tears for times like this," Millie assured her. "You just cry them all out."

CHAPTER

8

Working Prayers

Be joyful in hope, patient in affliction, faithful in prayer.

ROMANS 12:12

illie prayed for Mia and the baby as she walked up the hill to the hacienda, swinging her arms and walking briskly to combat the cold wind that had sprung up. The pale afternoon sun was simply no competition for the icy breath from the mountain peaks. Her nose was frozen and her ears ached from the wind by the time she arrived.

Charles and Don Rael were just dismounting as she strode up to the front steps. Don Rael was so covered in mud that Millie put her hand to her mouth, thinking there had been an accident.

"Buenos tardes, Señora," the mud creature said, his face splitting open in a smile. "I trust you had a pleasant day."

"I did, thank you. And did you . . . " Charles, standing behind Don Rael's shoulder, was mouthing something that might have been "don't ask," but Millie saw it too late. ". . . make the mountain tremble?" Charles silently smacked his hand to his forehead.

"We shook her to her roots!" Don Rael said. Then he launched into a description of drilling the stone in order to set the blast, while Millie bounced on her toes, shivered, and tried to pay attention. A full fifteen minutes of nodding and smiling had not moved the story beyond the placing of the blasting powder. Finally, Don Rael paused and Millie thought that he would at least move the story inside, but it proved a false hope. The presence of the stone steps inspired him to act out the placing of the blasting powder. Twenty cold minutes had passed and the steps were demolished in an imaginary explosion before his eyes focused on reality once more. "But you are tired after your day! Why do you insist on standing in the cold?" he asked. "Come inside! You must tell my nephew," he said, bounding up the stairs, "that the steam pumps are worth every penny that his father spent. The Rael mines will be the richest in the nation! On second thought," he said as he ushered them through the door, "I will tell him myself, after I clean up."

"That is a man with a passion," said Charles, shaking his head as Don Rael disappeared down the hall. "I tried to warn you not to ask him."

Millie giggled. "Is that what you were doing? I thought you'd been struck by a sudden headache."

"In fact, I felt one coming on. I have heard the complete story three times now, and I suspect we will hear it again at dinner," said Charles.

"We won't have to wait that long. He wants to share it with Otis. You must admit, it was quite interesting the first time," Millie said, smiling with amusement.

"Uh-huh." Charles took her cloak as they entered the parlor, hanging it on the coat tree by the door.

"How was your tea?" Otis asked, as Millie hurried to the stove. She gave one mighty shiver to shake the last of the cold air from her clothes before she replied.

"Shall we say I have learned that I can do all things through Christ who strengthens me, and leave it at that?"

"No!" Otis said. "I have been trapped inside these walls all day," he glanced over his shoulder, "with far too many thoughts of my own. I want to hear how each of you spent your day—every detail."

"In that case," Charles said, "I have very good news for you. Your uncle will be by to tell you about his day at the mines. As for my news, Tomas has agreed to spend two hours a day teaching me the Quechua language. I have my first sermon planned, and I'm hoping to be preaching it before spring."

"Where?" Otis asked. "I don't think the clinic waiting room will be large enough for a church. There is not a building in town that would suit."

"Jesus preached on a hillside," Charles said. "I can do the same."

"I would offer to play accompaniment," Millie said, holding her hands over the stove to warm them, "but I doubt Angela will allow her piano to be hauled up a hill. Perhaps Tomas can bring his shepherd's pipes." The young man often played the pipes when the workers took a break, and Millie thought it was some of the loveliest music she had ever heard.

"As for my day . . ." She described her surprise party and the time she had spent with Mia. "And I believe you are right, Dr. Landreth. We are making progress, at least in making friends and showing Jesus' love. Why are you making that face? Are you in pain?"

"Guinea pig?" Charles's grimace deepened. "You ate a guinea pig?"

"Two, actually," Millie said. "They were small. But I had to. I could not bear to offend her. And how was your noodling, Otis?"

"Ah!" He picked up a paper from the table beside him. "Ah! The result of my inquiry. . . " He put the paper down and ran his fingers through his hair. "Don't laugh, Charles, but it has left me wanting to hide under a blanket. I'm sure I shouldn't feel that way, but I have had the shivers all afternoon. I'm terribly glad you are back!"

"What was your inquiry?" Charles asked.

"The question was, is witchcraft real or is it simply the-atrics?" Millie glanced at her husband, wondering if it had been on his mind as well.

"You, Charles, said that it was theatrics," Otis went on. "Millie believed that it was theatrics with something more, something sinister behind the curtain. And I—I have a broken leg. So I went to my Bible."

"And what have you found?" Charles asked, looking just as interested as Millie felt. "That Wanunu has no power, I'll wager."

"Yes . . . and no," Otis said. "It was clear to me right away that in and of herself she had no power to cause me harm. Just as a Christian who has the gift of miracles does not do the miracles himself. God does them. So in a way you are right, Charles."

"In a way?" Charles frowned, and Otis gave a tiny shrug.

"The things Wanunu does—they have no power. The real question that I had was, can Satan physically hinder or harm a Christian?"

"And have you found an answer?" Millie asked.

"I believe I have," Otis said. "In Thessalonians Paul says that he wanted to visit them, but Satan prevented it. Just as I wanted to keep visiting the village and telling stories to the children, but this broken leg will prevent it for a time."

Charles was clearly not convinced. "But we don't know that Paul was physically hindered or harmed. It could have been circumstances."

"Ah!" Otis held up a finger. "That is true. But this Scripture," Millie looked over his shoulder to see him running his finger along the lines of 2 Corinthians 12:7, "is more clear: 'To keep me from becoming conceited because of these surpassingly great revelations, there was given me a thorn in my flesh, a messenger of Satan, to torment me. Three times I pleaded with the Lord to take it away from me. But he said to me, "My grace is sufficient for you, for my power is made perfect in weakness." ' " He looked up at them. "Clearly, this affected Paul's flesh. And clearly it was from Satan. It does not say that it happened because he was not walking with the Lord, or because he was sinning."

Charles rubbed his chin. "Satan did harm Paul's flesh, but God allowed it."

"God used for good what Satan meant for evil," Otis said. "My leg belongs to Jesus."

Millie felt a prickle of answered prayer, and she was sure Jesus was smiling at her. Otis gazed at his toes peeking out from under the blanket. "I am sure that He would not have allowed me to hurt so much unless great good could come of it. Satan meant this for evil, but God will use it for good, as He did with Paul's thorn in the side. I am content to trust Him."

"You amaze me, Otis!" Millie said.

"Yes, er . . . well. I spent the better part of the day praying and reading my way to this conclusion. And if I had left it there . . . but I didn't. I kept after the subject, and well . . . I found—demons."

"You spent the whole day thinking of these things?" Charles asked. "No wonder you have the shivers."

Otis lowered his paper. "I confess, I have been about this all day, practically alone, and—"

"Practically?" Charles inquired.

"Rosarita did bring me a snack now and then. Just little bits of this and that," he said. Millie looked at the stack of dishes on the table. "By the afternoon," Otis hurried on, "I found that the New Testament spoke often of demons. Jesus was tempted by Satan before His ministry began . . ."

Millie's Fiery Trial

"Jesus cast demons out of people," Millie said.

"Well, er, yes. That's true. But demons can make people sick, give them seizures, or give them uncommon strength. They can also cause people to hurt themselves—even throw themselves in the fire." Otis looked up. "And they seem to be able to perform actions through those who serve them. Paul encountered a man named Simon who did miracles through sorcery, and a slave girl who told the future by the power of an evil spirit. When it was cast out, the power went away. It seems almost as if they were a kind of . . . sickness."

"That Jesus cured," Charles pointed out. "And gave His disciples the authority to cure as well. It also says in Acts chapter 10 that God anointed Jesus with the Holy Spirit, and that Jesus went around healing all who were under the power of the devil, because God was with Him."

"I know," Otis said. "And I read the verses in Ephesians 6 about wearing the armor of God and standing against the devil's schemes, but I do not understand how—"

There was a knock at the door and Rosarita appeared, smiling shyly at Otis as she carried in a tray of freshly fried donuts.

"Er . . . thank you," Otis said. "Gratzi."

"Gracias," Millie corrected. "Gratzi is Italian."

"It is? I have been saying it all day, and she didn't tell me." Otis's face turned pink. "She's been bringing me platter after platter of food, despite my efforts to stop her," he said nervously, under his breath.

Rosarita turned at the door, smiled at Otis one last time, and winked as she closed the door behind her. Charles and Millie exchanged glances at this.

"My word!" Otis said. "You must help me, Charles!"

"Happily," Charles said, scooping up a handful of donuts. "We are commanded to share one another's burdens."

"Not with the food," Otis sputtered. "You know very well what I mean!"

"Mmmmm. She is a very good cook, Otis," Charles said, teasing his friend.

"I am not looking for a good cook!" Otis declared, "or any other kind of cook for that matter. I would run but . . ." he waved at his leg.

"Never mind the two of you," Millie said, reaching for a small donut herself. "I will speak to the smitten Rosarita and explain the situation to her."

"But—" Otis was pink again. "Be gentle. She is very young, and . . . "

"Could not resist your curls and charming smile?" Millie teased. "Charles, if you eat all of those donuts, you will have no appetite for supper." Charles put one of the donuts back.

"As I was saying," Otis was blushing furiously now and eager to change the subject. "We are commanded to stand against the devil's schemes, but how? It's all very good to say, 'put on the armor of God,' but what does that mean? I've been trying for two hours at least—even imagining myself putting on a metal hat and such. I am sure that they are out to get me, and I don't feel a bit better, not a bit. What happens if I forget my armor? What if my breastplate is not thick enough?"

"Otis," Millie said, pulling a chair closer to the fire so she could face him. "I'm not sure you are looking at this in the right way. I have given this more than a little thought since we came here. This is what God told me: 'Be strong in the Lord and in his mighty power.' It is His spiritual armor, not your physical armor. Paul is echoing a verse from Isaiah 59."

"I love that whole chapter," Charles said, picking up the Bible from the table beside Otis's chair. " 'Surely the arm of the Lord is not too short to save,' " he read, " 'nor his ear too dull to hear. But your iniquities have separated you from your God; your sins have hidden his face from you, so that he will not hear. . . . Justice is far from us, and righteousness does not reach us. We look for light, but all is darkness; for brightness, but we walk in deep shadows. Like the blind we grope along the wall, feeling our way like men without eyes.' "

"That sounds like the people of Orofino," Otis said. "Or me a few months ago, for that matter."

"God was not willing to leave His children in that terrible state," Millie said. "He came to save us."

"That part is in verse 17." Charles ran his finger down the page. " 'He put on righteousness as his breastplate, and the helmet of salvation on his head; he put on the garments of vengeance and wrapped himself in zeal as in a cloak. According to what they have done, so will he repay wrath to his enemies and retribution to his foes,' " he quoted.

"He did not put on His armor because He was afraid that He would be attacked," Millie said. "He dressed for war. His people were lost, afraid, and unable to save themselves, so He came to rescue them. Jesus did not come to make war on men. His wrath is against Satan and his demons, for what they have done to the children of Adam. The battle has been won. Their doom is assured, and we are eternally safe in our Lord. And it is His armor that we wear."

"That is a comforting thought," Otis said.

The door opened and Rosarita appeared again—this time bearing an offering of cookies and tea with only one teacup, Millie noticed.

"Thank you, dear," Millie said, taking the tray from her, and shooing her back out the door.

"You may be right," Charles said, watching Rosarita as she left the room. "You may have a problem with that young lady. Pass the cookies."

"I told you," Otis sighed. "Could I have a cup of tea, Millie?"

"I believe the armor Paul speaks of in Ephesians," Millie said as she poured, "is simply this: to understand what Jesus has done for us and to believe and abide in Him. If we do that, our armor is complete."

Don Rael chose that moment to make his appearance—clean, but just as eager to tell his story once again. Millie had to agree that it was not as interesting the second time, and she and Charles slipped quietly out of the room.

Otis was excited when they returned to the room later. "I have figured it out!" he said. "We are to set the people free by preaching the Word and praying. That is how we go to war—see, it's in verse 17: 'Take the helmet of salvation and the sword of the Spirit, which is the word of God. And pray in the Spirit on all occasions with all kinds of prayers and requests.' "

They spent the evening reading Scripture aloud, seeking out God's promises, and presenting their Heavenly Father with all kinds of requests and prayers for the men, women, and children of Bolivia. With great passion they prayed that the lost Bolivians would have their eyes opened and the opportunity to hear the Word of God. They asked God to help the people of Bolivia see through the lies and deception of the enemy. At times, Millie had tears on her cheeks as she prayed for freedom for the captives, and her heart felt ablaze with a holy fire until she was sure it was burning with God's own love for the people of Bolivia who didn't know Him.

"Let us preach boldly, God," Charles prayed, "proclaiming Your truth to every soul here. Give us the words to fearlessly make known the mystery of the Gospel. Give us words in Quechua, Lord. Make our minds sharp and our tongues agile to pronounce the words that will tell them of You."

"Lord," Millie prayed, "open their eyes. By Your power, roll back the darkness here and let these people see through the devil's lies. Let them see the truth. Banish all forms of evil in this city." They continued to pray, adding special requests for people by name, until they could think of no more.

"And Father God," Otis said at last, "I do realize that there are demons in this darkness. But Your book is full of angels as well. I would really rather meet one of those, if I must come face-to-face with any such creatures."

Millie and Charles echoed his "amen." When Charles helped Millie up from her knees, she was surprised to see that they had been praying for hours, and morning was not far away.

Millie waited until she had finished her salteñas the next morning before she broached the subject of Otis with Rosarita. She soon found that while her language skills were adequate for saying "pass the potatoes" or "is it too hot?" they were completely inadequate for the task at hand. After two attempts that left the girl baffled or blushing, Millie enlisted Savannah's aid to explain that Otis was not currently interested in finding a wife.

The result of this interview was that Otis, while not as well fed, was much more comfortable in his convalescence. He was bewildered, however, by the sudden gales of giggles that Savannah seemed to have developed in his presence.

Charles returned from the clinic that afternoon to help Millie deliver the soup.

"I would really like to examine Mia," he explained. "It would be nice to know how long until the baby is due. And since she is talking to you, perhaps she will allow it."

Millie thought this was a very good idea, but when they arrived, Mia did not agree. She hid under a blanket, refusing to come out until Charles left.

"There is time," Millie said. "I'm sure we have at least two months."

"But as a doctor—" Charles started. Millie put her hand on his arm. "Women attend these matters all over the world," she assured him. "I will tell you if we need you. Does Orofino seem . . . different to you this morning?"

"People are smiling a lot," Charles said. "But I assumed they always smiled at you."

It was true they were smiling more, and seemed friendlier as well, not just that day, but every day. It was as if they had turned a corner, or reached the top of a hill, and the traveling was easier on the other side. The women of Orofino began not only to smile at Millie, but to take her arms in their own and greet her with a kiss, just as they greeted one another. If Charles happened to be with her, the men would greet him with a warm *abrazo*, a hug, a firm handshake, and several pats on the shoulder.

Even Otis's broken leg produced a blessing. Though he could not run his Sunday school, Tupac often crept into the

parlor to hear stories, and Millie saw the boy retelling them to his goggle-eyed playmates behind the garden wall.

Angela spent more and more time with her nephew, as well. Otis was very bold in proclaiming the Gospel to his aunt. Every day she would listen for a time and then go back to her room, or ask Millie to push her in the garden until the chill drove them inside, only to come again the next day and listen a little longer. Faith seemed to be growing in her like the dawn, a mere hope of light before the sun edged across the horizon, until she was discussing the Scriptures Otis read eagerly. And with faith, life seemed to come back into her, and illness to retreat. Much to Millie's delight, she even paced the floor when discussions grew lively. Charles could only shake his head and smile.

"Sometimes," he said, "God heals all at once, and sometimes He takes His time."

"I believe you are right," Millie said. "And He must have His reasons. If Angela could dance today, she would dance rather than read the Bible with Otis. And speaking of reasons, I would consider this God using poor Otis's broken leg for good, wouldn't you?"

"I must confess I would," Charles said.

Angela was not the only one changing. One day, to Millie's surprise, Mia left her house and followed along behind her like a silent shadow as she delivered soup and bread. Soon she was sweeping floors or playing with children while Millie tended the sick or old.

"The Ladies Aid Society apparently has two members now," Millie said to her husband. "Mia loves to help others."

Charles only sighed. "I wish I could say I was seeing the breakthroughs you and Otis seem to be. I work with Tomas every day. We can communicate well enough to talk about

Jesus, and he is helping me with my sermon. He must have listened to it a hundred times now, but still he seems no closer to accepting the Lord. Every time I ask him about it, he says he is thinking. No one in Orofino has accepted the Lord, Millie."

"Remember Galatians 6:9, 'Let us not become weary in doing good, for at the proper time we will reap a harvest if we do not give up,' " Millie quoted.

"Yes, yes," Charles said. "And I know we were called here. But I would like to see the fruit."

With the coming of June, winter settled in, but it was not as cold as Millie expected. There were no drifts of snow for sledding, or iced ponds for skating. It was a dreary chill, punctuated by sudden storms of icy rain that made walking in the hills precarious. The chilly breath of the mountains managed to find its way through the tucks and folds of the warmest cloak or coat. Millie had spent far too long indoors before she discovered a corner of the garden where the walls not only blocked the wind, but also absorbed the heat of the sun, making the spot almost balmy. Millie liked to take her prayer journal and do her letter writing here. Tupac and Savannah would sometimes join her, Savannah playing with Pilpintu while Tupac watched Millie's quill in amazement.

"What are you writing?" Tupac asked one day.

"I'm describing all the people of Orofino," Millie answered.

"Can you leave Wanunu out of your book?" he said. "She should not be in there."

Millie's Fiery Trial

"I have not seen her for some time," Millie said. "Where has she been?"

"She went up the mountain," Tupac said. "The day after Mia started to talk, she went like dogs were nipping her heels."

The day after we prayed, Millie thought.

"She has been gone a long time," Tupac said. "Maybe she'll never come back." He smiled happily at the thought.

CHAPTER

9

Bad Tidings

He will have no fear of bad news;
his heart is steadfast, trusting
in the Lord.

PSALM 112:7

Bad Tidings

*O*n Millie's next visit to the clinic, the roof, doors, and windows had been installed, and when she saw the bare floors and walls, her fingers positively itched to have rags for rag rugs or fabric for curtains. She could purchase rags at the market, but there was nothing suitable for curtains, and so she left the windows bare.

This led to rather uncomfortable moments, as the village people liked to stand outside and stare in, as if Charles and Millie were creatures on display at the zoo, as they unloaded boxes and arranged books, journals, bottles, and tins on the shelves.

"We are open for business!" Charles said at last.

Millie opened the door and came face-to-face with an old man.

"Hello," she said, stepping back as his friends pushed him forward. He was very thin, with shaggy white hair and a sad, wrinkled face, which was badly swollen on one side. "Won't you come in? The doctor will see you immediately."

Charles led him into the examining room, and the entire group of his friends trooped in after him, crowding around to see what Charles would do. Charles settled the old fellow in a chair and motioned for him to open his mouth by opening his own. His friends called encouragement to him, opening their own mouths also, until he slowly complied. Millie had to turn her head away at the smell.

"Just as I thought," Charles said, peering into the maw. "An infected tooth. We are going to have to pull it. I'm surprised the poor fellow has any teeth at all, at his age. They sprinkle lime on the coca leaf while they chew it, and it eats the teeth."

To say nothing of turning them green, Millie thought.

Charles opened a drawer, humming to himself, and took out a shiny new pair of pliers. The old man's eyes grew huge, and a murmur went through the crowd.

"They are the best in modern dentistry," Charles assured the old gentleman. For some reason, this did not reassure the patient in the least. He came up out of the chair and made a dash for the door, but his friends caught him and hauled him back and held him down.

"Now, that won't be necessary," Charles said, waving them away. The old man's eyes were on the long-handled pliers, but his hand was on his aching jaw. Huge tears spilled down his cheeks and disappeared into the wrinkles. Finally he opened his mouth again.

"That's the spirit!" Charles said, encouraging him. "You will feel much better when that tooth is gone. Hmmmm. The chair is too tall. I won't have the leverage I need, and I can hardly ask him to sit on the floor. What I need is a stool."

There was no stool, but the box from which Millie had been unloading supplies was still at hand. He upended it beside the chair and climbed on top. This brought a murmur of approval from the bystanders.

"Be careful, Charles," Millie said. "Doctors are scarce around here."

"You might put your hands on his shoulders," Charles said, "just in case he tries to bolt again."

Millie did, and felt the shudder go through him as Charles gripped the tooth with his extraction pliers and pulled. Nothing happened. "It's a tough one," Charles said. "I'm going to have to give it all I've got. One . . . two . . . three!"

Bad Tidings

The man gave a great shout, and Charles toppled backwards off the stool, ending up on his back. He sat up, examining the remains of the molar. "Roots intact!" he announced, and the crowd against the wall cheered.

The man looked surprised. He felt his jaw, then smiled a huge, green, snaggletoothed smile. He sat quietly as Millie packed the side of his mouth with cotton to stop the bleeding. Then he held out his hand. "I think he wants his tooth back," Millie said.

Charles obliged him, dropping it into his hand. It was examined by all of his friends, and he was clapped on the back. He nodded, accepting that he was the hero of the hour, grinning and drooling, shaking Charles's hand over and over before he left.

The clinic did such a brisk business in tooth extraction for two weeks following that Charles was forced to teach Tomas to pull them, leaving him free to see other patients.

"He can pull them more quickly than I can," Charles admitted one day as they walked through the market looking for a sturdy three-legged stool. "That young man would make a fine doctor."

"I think he would make a fine husband," Millie said.

"You already have a husband," Charles said.

"I am not speaking of myself," Millie said. "I am speaking of Mia. I am not the only one who thinks so, either. I believe he thinks so himself."

"You don't say!" Charles stopped to examine a stool, but the legs wobbled. He shook his head and they walked on.

"I do. Who do you think was taking care of Mia before I found her? Tomas and Tupac, that's who," Millie replied.

"They will care for anything that is hurt or lost," said Charles.

"Yes," Millie said. "But when he isn't helping you, did you know that he sits on her hearth and plays his shepherd's pipes?"

"She lets him in the house?" Charles asked, surprised.

"Not at first. Tupac could come in, but Tomas could not. He used to sit on her doorstep and play." Millie sighed with the notion of young love.

"Circumstantial evidence," Charles said, playfully challenging his wife's assumptions.

"Really . . . Then would you take the statement of a witness? Tupac told me that Tomas is in love," she said triumphantly.

"Hearsay," Charles said, but he was smiling. "It will never hold up in a court of law."

"I believe it is the court of Mia's heart that matters," Millie bantered back.

"Does he stand a chance in that court?" retorted Charles.

"If he *courts*, he stands a chance," Millie smiled, pleased with her own play on words. Then, more thoughtfully, she said, "I think his love could help mend her broken heart. I would like to see them both come to know the Lord first. Mia has a sweet spirit, and Tomas—"

"Ah!" Charles finally found the stool he was looking for, but it was currently beneath the broad beam of a woman selling cheeses. It took a good deal of bartering before they left the market with the stool and six cheeses.

The first of July dawned with a storm on the mountain, reaching down with gusts of icy fingers to test the doors and windows of the hacienda.

Bad Tidings

"I think I will spend the day at the clinic," Charles said. "I don't know that the weather will permit people to come tomorrow." Millie bundled up to accompany him, taking her writing along. It was far too unpleasant to ride, so they hitched the horse to the surrey and bumped over the roads.

Charles's patients must have had the same thought, as a line was waiting outside the clinic door. Charles tied the horse in the shelter formed by the north wall of the clinic and the hill, with a nosebag of oats and a blanket on its back, while Millie opened the doors. The people all crowded inside the small waiting room, filling the chairs, sitting on the floor, or standing against the walls.

Charles worked his way through them, sending them home with a bottle of cough syrup for the children, a splint on a fractured thumb, sometimes a piece of candy, but always a prayer.

Millie kept the fire burning in the stove and helped whenever she could, welcoming the steady trickle of patients who came in the door. By the time the last patient left, light was fading.

"Seems like everything hit at once," Charles said, as he lit two lamps. "I've never seen it so busy before." He started putting his examination room in order.

Millie sat down at the desk to record the pills, lotions, and syrups that had been used. *Someone is watching me.* A quick glance around the room showed her that she was alone. Nonetheless, she moved her chair to the other side of the desk, so that her back was against the wall, and she felt more comfortable. It was not possible for anyone to be behind her, but the feeling would not go away. Millie thought of calling to Charles in the other room, but the sooner his examining room and books were in order, the sooner they could go home.

Someone is watching from the window. Her nib stopped moving. Who would be watching in the dark? *Pish-tosh. It's far too late for anyone to be at the window. The village people are home in bed . . . unless . . .*

"Hello," Millie called. "Do you need help?"

"No," Charles answered from the other room, obviously thinking she was speaking to him.

"I meant the person who is outside." Millie stood up and took a step toward the window. It was a face, wasn't it? Suddenly, fear stabbed through her. Maybe it wasn't a human face at all. She wanted to cry out, but her voice was caught in her throat. Eyes like burning embers looked into her own. "Charles!" She managed to gasp. He came into the room quickly.

"There was something out there." She pointed at the window. "It was looking in. It had . . . horrible eyes." Charles was out the door in an instant, and Millie picked up the lantern and followed him.

"There's no one here," Charles said.

"I'm sure there was!" Millie said.

"Perhaps it was an animal. Their eyes can easily glow in the light of a lantern. We will check for tracks tomorrow," Charles said. "Until then, I think we'd best go home."

Millie was very glad of his arm around her on the ride home. She was uneasy all night and happy for the company of Tupac and Savannah when she visited Mia the next day. The storm was still promising to descend on the town, but so far it had done nothing but huff and puff.

Still, Millie was glad when Mia offered to share a pot of tea. She could not shake her sense of unease. Savannah and Tupac were playing happily in the corner, a game in which they tossed a stone in the air, then snatched up as many beans as possible before catching it again, a game Mia had taught them.

Millie had just accepted a cup when a shadow filled the room. Millie turned to see Wanunu silhouetted against the light. Mia saw her as well, and cowered back, dropping the teakettle, which clattered across the floor, spilling boiling water. Savannah and Tupac jumped up to avoid being scalded.

"You are not welcome here," Millie said. "This is Mia's house. Get out."

Wanunu stuck her hand in her pocket, pulled it out dramatically, and opened it to reveal a pile of powder. She blew on it, sending the tiny particles spinning in the air.

"I said," Millie took a step closer.

"Ah-ah-ah-choo!" Mia sneezed, then clapped her hand over her mouth and nose, her eyes huge and frightened. Wanunu snatched something from the air and cackled with joy as she stuck it in her pocket.

Tupac gasped, and Wanunu smiled, drew her shawl around her, and stalked away, head held high. Tupac ran outside after her, grabbing up a rock. Millie ran out and caught his arm before he could throw it.

"Tupac!" Millie said. "What just happened?"

"Wanunu took a soul," he said. "The soul of Mia's baby."

"She just sneezed," Millie said. "The old woman blew pepper in her face."

But when Millie and Tupac went back inside, they found Mia crying inconsolably. Millie sat with her until the tears had dried up, then she picked up her bonnet and cloak.

"Where are you going?" Tupac asked.

"To Wanunu's house," Millie said.

"Her house?" he shook his head. "That is not a good idea, Millie. She will not give the soul back."

Millie's Fiery Trial

"Yes, it is," Millie said. "I have a few things to say to that woman. And she does not have the baby's soul."

Tupac shook his head pityingly and laid his hand on Millie's arm. "I'll go with you, then," he said, as if she were going to her doom.

"No, you won't." Millie looked around. "You take Savannah home. Tell Charles that I will be right along."

Millie marched through the streets of Orofino, trying to contain her anger, and succeeding so poorly that she had to stop at the corner of the market square to take a deep breath and say a quick prayer. She reminded herself of her husband's words, *We are not fighting Wanunu. We are wrestling with the evil powers that are working through her.* Jesus, she prayed, *this evil will not be overcome by my might or power, but by Your Spirit. Let Your Spirit flow through me!*

Everyone knew where Wanunu lived—it was one of the nicest houses in town, with fresh thatch on the roof and smoke always curling from the chimney hole.

"Wanunu!" Millie called, banging on the door. There was no answer. She knocked on the door again, but when there was no answer she pushed it open and stepped inside. The hairs on Millie's neck rippled as if they had been brushed by an invisible hand. It was worse than walking into the witches' market, as the air felt thick and unclean. The old woman squatted on her heels in the back of the room beside a small, smoky fire, breathing the fumes and rocking.

It was very warm and even damp inside the room, and smelled of . . . reptile. There were stick cages in the back, and things coiled inside of them. How did she keep the place warm enough so they stayed awake in the winter?

"You will stop torturing that girl with your tricks!" Millie said firmly. "You are a fake and a liar. You blew pepper in

Mia's face to make her sneeze, that's all . . . and you cannot steal a baby's soul!"

"She does not speak your language."

Millie whirled to see Señor Torrez stepping from the shadows, and her flesh crawled again. "But I will translate if you wish."

"I do." Millie folded her arms and watched as he spoke.

Wanunu lifted her eyes to Millie, eyes that were flat and dead as a serpent's. A slow, knowing smile spread across her face, and she began to speak in a singsong chant, passing her hand through the smoke of the brazier before her as she did so. Her eyes held Millie's as Señor Torrez translated.

Millie felt supernatural strength sustain her. *Greater is He that is in me,* she said over and over to herself. Millie locked eyes with Wanunu and could almost feel the clash between two kingdoms—the kingdom of light and the kingdom of darkness. For a brief moment Millie sensed in Wanunu a wavering. She saw the smirk on Wanunu's face become a look of fear, and Millie knew the dark forces in Wanunu were quaking at the presence of God's Spirit.

Señor Torez stepped in quickly to distract the showdown, and immediately the evil look returned to Wanunu's eyes. "She says you do not know the ways of the Quechua. Your God does not know their ways or speak their language. You are already defeated, and as proof of this, you will get very bad news, Señora Landreth. Very bad. Prepare yourself."

"Pish-tosh," Millie said. "You tell her to stay away from Mia." Millie turned to go, and Señor Torrez walked to the door as well. "I did not ask for your company," she said.

"I did not ask for yours, either," he said with a shrug, "but we are going in the same direction, and . . . I would speak with you."

Millie did not see how she could avoid it, so she inclined her head. "You are a follower of Pachamama, are you not?" Millie asked as they walked through the streets.

"Yes," he said.

"And when you left us in La Paz, you went to the witches' market to buy things for Wanunu."

"There are . . . items . . . there that cannot be found in Orofino. My grandmother had need of them," he replied evenly.

Millie stopped and turned to him. "Your grandmother?"

"Si. I was not threatening you the day I told you about the snake. I was warning you. There are powerful things here that you do not understand. I tell you this because I have two allegiances. One is to the Hacienda de Rael, and it is for Don Rael's sake that I warn you. The other is much older. I was dedicated at my birth to Pachamama, as was my grandmother. When she dies, I will be the brujo of this village. It is a great honor and responsibility. Wanunu has carried it for many years."

"And Don Rael knows this?" Millie asked.

"Don Rael is at peace with the old ways. He allows the sacrifices. But he should not have allowed you and your husband to come here. Unless you choose to learn our ways . . . "

"Jesus is not at peace with the old ways," Millie said. "And so we cannot be either. What your grandmother just did to Mia was cruel, deceitful, and wrong."

"Mia has offended the gods. She must be punished, or the whole village will suffer," he said.

"And Wanunu decides who has caused offense?" she asked.

"The gods speak to her when she goes up on the mountain. Sometimes she is gone for weeks, but when she comes down, she has great power. I will go to the mountain with her soon. It will be time for me to inherit."

"I will pray, for your sake," Millie said as she left him at the door, "that that never happens."

"Señora Landreth," he called after her, "I am truly sorry about your news."

⌒⌐

"Charles," Millie said, storming into the bedroom, "you will not believe—" but she stopped at the look on his face.

"What is it? Is Otis well?"

"Otis is fine," he said. "Sit down, Millie. There is a letter from Marcia."

"From home? But what—"

"Sit down, dearest. I will read it to you." Millie sank onto the bed, and Charles sat beside her.

"Our Darling Fan has gone to be with the Lord," he read. Millie shook her head. *Fan, gone to be with the Lord! No! She's safe at Keith Hill with Mamma and Pappa.*

"A young family stopped in town," Charles read on. "They were ill, and Fan and Celestia Ann took food to their wagon. Fan stayed to care for the sick children. Typhoid is a terrible sickness, Millie. Fan was already sick before we realized what it was. Dr. Chetwood could hardly quarantine a wagon, and we would not leave our darling there, so we sent Adah and Annis to stay with Zillah, and brought them all to Keith Hill.

Millie's Fiery Trial

"You must know that Fan wanted to be a missionary like her older sister, and travel to foreign lands. Instead, she walked into the valley of the shadow of death to save those who were perishing. She took two little souls with her to Heaven, dearest, praying for them on their sick beds. They were all so weak, and the poor parents out of their minds with fever. Fan held the little ones close while they died, and then she closed her eyes. I'm sure she held two little hands in her own as they walked toward the Lord, so they would not feel so alone. And they won't be alone forever, for the parents came to the Lord at your sister's funeral.

"Pray for your father, Dearest. So many people have tried to console your Pappa by saying he should think of the children he has left, plenty to fill his house and heart. But in a father's heart, eight minus one is not plenty. It is seven and one forever gone, forever missing. There is a Fan-shaped hole in his heart, and he can hardly bear it. Know that I pray for you, and would comfort you if I could in this time. I will write again when I can, as soon as the tears stop flowing."

"When?" Millie whispered. Charles read the date at the top of the letter. Millie put her hand over her mouth. *Months ago! When we set foot in Bolivia, my sister lay ill, dying. When I laughed at Fan's letter, hearing her voice in the words, that voice was already stilled. Fan is dead, dead, dead.*

Charles took her in his arms and Millie cried until her sobs were dry. But not even an ocean of tears could wash away the words on the page.

CHAPTER

10

Saving Grace

*I am the resurrection and the
life. He who believes in me
will live, even though
he dies.*

JOHN 11:25

*A*ll night an icy wind from the mountain seemed to batter the windows of the hacienda. Charles held Millie while she cried. It was well past time for dinner before she was able to talk, telling Charles of Wanunu's trickery and prophecy and the fact that Señor Torrez was her grandson.

"It was not Pachamama who took Fan's life," Millie said, "though Wanunu would believe that it was, and take credit for it."

"Of course it wasn't." Charles handed her a fresh handkerchief to add to the pile at her side, and Millie blew her nose. "Someone could have told her," said Charles. "The letter was not sealed, after all, and was carried by a fellow who works for Señor Torrez. Much of the evil in this world is done by men, Millie dear. I will go to see Mia tomorrow."

"She will not let you in. I'm sure that Tomas is watching over her."

Somewhere in the small hours of the night, Millie realized that Charles had fallen asleep, his arms still around her. Millie cried again silently, great burning tears as if her heart were ripped open. She wanted to pray for her Pappa, and for Mamma, and Mia and her baby, for the people of Orofino who were trapped in darkness, but the pain was so deep she could not find the words.

Someone is praying. She could almost hear those words, almost understand . . . but not quite. Peace filled the room and Scriptures tumbled through her mind, bringing her comfort.

Hope that is seen is no hope at all. Who hopes for what he already has? But if we hope for what we do not yet have, we wait for it patiently. In the same way, the Spirit helps us in our weakness. We do not know what we ought to pray for, but the Spirit himself intercedes for us with groans that words cannot express. Millie tried to remember the rest of the passage from Romans 8, but could not. *Thank You, Holy Spirit,* she prayed. *Thank You for praying for me.* Peace surrounded and filled her. *Fan is with Jesus. Surely the Spirit has comforted Mamma and Pappa, as He is comforting me. And Mia will be* . . . Suddenly the verse came, *We know that in all things God works for the good of those who love him, who have been called according to his purpose. Yes, of course. That was it.*

***

"I look exactly like a rhinoceros," Millie said to her husband. "All nose."

"It is only a little red and—"

"Swollen." Millie said, interrupting him. "You were going to say swollen. It feels like a snout. And my eyes are beady little red bulbs."

"They are a tiny bit puffy," Charles said.

"Besides," Otis commented from his crutches, "God likes rhinoceroses."

Both Charles and Millie looked at him. "Otis, old man," Charles said, "if you ever do decide to marry, remind me that we need to have a talk."

"I'm going to wash my face again before we go to breakfast," Millie said.

When they reached the dining room at last, Don Rael and Angela both expressed their sympathy at Millie's loss. Savannah was looking at her big-eyed and solemn, but it was Señor Torrez's gaze that Millie felt.

"Thank you," Millie said, her eyes welling up against her will. "I do feel the loss keenly, but . . ." Here her eyes met those of the segundo. ". . . but I have an assurance that my sister is with our Lord and I will see her again. I am comforted by the fact that her life was not taken, but given."

"What do you mean?" Angela asked.

"We are each given one life to spend," Millie said. "Like a handful of precious gold coins. We can hoard it, or we can spend it for the good of others. Fan spent her life in the service of her Lord, and with it purchased four souls to be with Jesus forever."

"But still, you cry," said Señor Torrez. Everyone looked at him, uncertain of what to say. Millie felt Charles take her hand under the table.

"Of course I do," she said. "Even Jesus wept at the tomb of a friend. I weep for myself because I will miss her very much, and for my parents whose hearts hurt. But these tears will not last, and one day we will all be together. Jesus Himself will wipe the tears from our eyes."

"I think the weather will not allow a visit to the Hamra mine today," Don Rael said, clearly changing the subject. Millie was thankful, for though she knew every word she had said was true, her stomach was still so full of grief that she could not eat.

"Why don't you take a nap this morning?" Charles asked as they left the table. "I will spend time with Angela. I want to discuss a few things with her anyway. Her lungs sounded much clearer the last time I examined her, and I suspect she will be up and walking soon."

Millie took a deep breath. "Thank you, I think I will." The sleep that had eluded her all night seemed to be tugging at her now irresistibly, and she crawled under the covers and gave in. She awoke, still groggy, in late afternoon, and started to rise from the bed.

"What are you doing?" Charles asked.

"I need to take some food to Mia," Millie replied.

"Already done," Charles waved his hand. "I had Consuela make a big pot of soup, enough for two days, and sent it along with Tupac. The storm is still raging out there, and you, my dear, are going nowhere."

"If you insist, Dr. Landreth," Millie said, crawling back under the covers. "Charles, why are you just sitting there at this time of day?"

"I'm a little tired myself," Charles said.

The next time Millie woke it was morning again, and Charles was still sitting in the chair.

"Have you been there all this time?" she asked with a smile.

"More than I would have liked to have been," Charles said. "I seem to be having some difficulty with my feet." Millie rolled out of bed and knelt beside him. His ankles were swollen and red, hot to the touch. "It's happened before," Charles said, "and usually only lasts a day or two."

"When?" Millie said.

"A few times since we arrived. It really hasn't worried me much." He held up his hand and the fingers were swollen. "But it has always been my feet before, or my knees, and that has not caused too much difficulty."

"Does it hurt?" Millie asked, concerned.

"Not too much," he said. "It always comes with a headache, and I feel very weak for a day or two."

"Why didn't you tell me?" she asked softly.

"I have always been as healthy as a horse." He shrugged. "It wasn't too bad the first time, and I suppose I have become used to it."

"Can you walk?" she asked.

"With difficulty. I'm sure it will be better tomorrow, Millie."

"But what is it?" Millie persisted.

"I don't know," Charles said. "I have found nothing like it in any journal."

They prayed together and, to Millie's relief, Charles was better the next day, his hands and feet showing no signs of swelling or stiffness. "I told you," he said. "It leaves me a little tired, that's all."

The storm had subsided at last, leaving the sky scoured and the air cold and damp. When she was sure Charles was all right, Millie prepared a basket of bread, meat, and jam to take to Mia. Savannah begged to go along, and Angela gave her approval. They met Tupac coming up the hill as they came down. "How is your brother?" Millie asked. "Has he been watching over Mia for us?"

"Tomas was called up to the high pastures yesterday," Tupac said, "to tend an injured sheep. He did not come home. Sometimes he has to stay with the animals."

A slight tickle of worry wormed its way through Millie. "Did you see Mia yesterday?"

"Oh, yes," Tupac said. "But not yet today. I took her extra dung for her fire, and some wood that Tomas had found for her, because it was cold. She was in a very bad mood."

"Come with us. We'll make her feel better," said Millie.

"Slow down, Millie," Savannah said. "Why are you going so fast? I can't keep up with you."

Millie's Fiery Trial

"Take my hand," Millie said, moving the basket to her other arm. "It will help us hurry a little." She was relieved to see a finger of smoke curling from Mia's chimney, and slowed her pace a little. Chaska smiled and waved at her, but Millie only waved back.

"Mia, we're here," Millie called when they reached the doorway. There was no reply. Millie pulled the blanket door aside and walked in. "Mia?" The small room was quiet, the still-quiet of a tomb.

"Where did she go, Millie?" Savannah asked.

There were coals in the fire pit, and the teakettle hung over them. The water bucket was half full. The kettle Tupac had delivered soup in two days before was scrubbed clean, sitting by the door. Surely she had not gone far, as her blankets were still on the bed. No. One blanket was left on her bed.

"Millie, look!" Tupac pulled the blanket up to reveal something else on the bed. It looked like a little wax doll, pale and still.

"No!" Millie cried. The basket dropped to the floor as she ran to the bed. "Mia must have given birth in the night all alone, and then fled—but where? Into the storm? Because her baby was stillborn?"

"Wanunu," Tupac whispered.

The baby girl's hand was perfectly formed, but cold to the touch when Millie took it in her own. "No!" Millie said it again, a great anger rising up in her against the devil. *First Fan, and now this little innocent baby who has never opened her eyes.*

"Is . . . is the baby dead?" Savannah whispered. Millie could not answer her, but she laid her hand on the little chest . . . and felt a slow flutter.

Millie's heart leapt in reply. Any midwife could tell stories of babies who did not breathe right away, who even appeared to be dead. *If I had been here, I could have helped! Dear Lord Jesus, don't let me be too late!* She scooped the baby into her arms. The little body was too cold to keep the fragile life in it for long. She had to warm the infant, and quickly.

"Put fuel on the fire, Tupac." *Jesus, help me think. How do I start? The teakettle!* Millie held the baby close with one hand and snatched the kettle off the coals with the other. The handle was hot enough to burn her fingers, and when she opened the top, it was two-thirds full and steaming gently. "Praise God," she said, sticking her fingers in the water. "Too hot!"

"Savannah, bring the empty soup pot from the door," Millie said. Savannah acted quickly, and Millie poured the hot water in it, adding dippers from the water bucket until the water was warm but not too hot. Then she lowered the baby in the pot, holding her little head up with one hand and gently rubbing her body with the other. "Fill the teakettle halfway full," Millie said, "and put it on the fire."

Savannah did as she was told and then knelt beside Millie, her hands clasped. Slowly the blue of the baby's skin was fading as the warmth worked its way into her little body. The baby made a mewling sound, turned its head, and kicked feebly.

"That's right," Millie said. "You fuss at me all you want. You fuss, sweetheart!"

"Ayyyyiiiii!" She looked up at the scream. Chaska was standing over her, her eyes wild. She babbled something far too quickly for Millie to understand.

"Can you help—" Millie began, but the the woman turned and fled screaming down the street.

"She said you were cooking the baby," Tupac said, his eyes worried. "Are you cooking it?"

"No," Millie said. "But I can see how she would think so. Not many people warm babies in soup kettles, I suppose. As soon as the baby is warm we will take her to the hacienda. I can't care for her here. I need you to find Tomas and tell him what has happened. Someone needs to go after Mia, and tell her that her baby is alive."

The baby was moving more now, waving shaky arms in the air, her little hands open wide. Millie warmed the water around her again, adding water from the teakettle carefully. The baby seemed fully awake now, warm and pink. There had to be a way to get her to the hacienda.

"Turn around," Millie said, and Tupac and Savannah obediently turned their backs. Millie dried the baby as best she could with the corner of a blanket, unbuttoned her blouse, and slipped it in against her skin, pulling her blouse closed around it.

"Are we taking her home now?" Savannah asked, uncertain.

"Yes," Millie said confidently, wrapping the blanket around herself and the baby. "We must hurry. Tupac, find Tomas!" Tupac pulled on his hat and set off at a run. Millie could not run burdened as she was, but she walked as quickly as possible, Savannah trotting to keep up. The baby had stopped moving when she reached the hacienda. *Let her just be sleeping*, Millie prayed. *Just sleeping.*

"Millie, what on earth?" Charles was standing on the front porch when she arrived, speaking with Otis. "Is everything all right?"

"No," Millie said, barely keeping the sob from her voice. "Charles, I need you!"

Charles was down the steps and to her side in an instant. He half carried her into the house, brushing past Otis on his way. "What's wrong?" Millie heard his question and the alarm in his voice, but it was Savannah who answered.

"It's the baby!" the little girl said. Otis gasped.

"To the kitchen, Charles," Millie said. "It's warmest there."

Consuela and Rosarita looked up as they came in. Charles set Millie on her feet, and pulled the blanket off her. She opened her shirt and took the baby out. It looked at her with murky baby eyes. "She's alive!" Millie cried, relieved.

"Hello, sweetheart," Charles said, taking her from Millie so she could button her blouse. He held the child close as Millie explained about finding her, and warming her in the kettle. Consuela tsked and fussed, bringing a clean towel to wrap the baby. Charles managed the affair without letting go of the little one.

"I don't know where Mia has gone," Millie said at last.

"Keeping you warm will be the chief thing," Charles said to the baby. "You surprised us all by coming too soon. But we'll find your mother. We will find her. Let's just walk over here by the stove."

"Let me take her, Charles," Millie said, as Otis hobbled into the room.

"Not so fast," Charles said, holding the baby up. "Look, Otis! It's a girl!"

Otis toppled, hitting the floor with a solid thud.

CHAPTER

11

More Threats

The eternal God is your refuge, and underneath are the everlasting arms. He will drive out your enemy before you, saying, "Destroy him!"

DEUTERONOMY 33:27

*C*harles handed the baby back to Millie and knelt by his friend's side.

"He fainted," he said, "but I don't think he broke anything this time. He'll be all right."

The back door burst open and Tupac came in, a bucket in his hand. Tomas was right behind him. At least Millie *thought* it was Tomas. He had obviously taken a beating. One eye was swollen shut; the other was black. His lips were split and puffy.

"Goat's milk," Tupac said, offering the bucket. Consuela took it, carrying it to Millie while Rosarita shut the door.

"What happened?" Charles asked, leaving Otis in order to examine Tomas.

"They came for him yesterday," Tupac said as Charles looked at the cuts. "Two men from up the mountain. They said they had an injured sheep, and so he went with them. But when they came to the mountain, there was no sheep. They beat him and threw him down a mine. Maybe they thought that he was dead. But he came home."

"Why would they do such a thing?" asked Charles.

"They said he must not help Mia anymore," Tupac said.

"This could use some stitches," Charles said.

"Did you tell him Mia was gone?" Millie asked. Tomas brushed Charles away and moved to Millie's side, walking with a noticeable limp.

"He said the baby needed food first," Tupac said, "and then he would find Mia."

"He is right." Millie dipped her finger in the milk, and while it was not warm, at least it was not cold. She put her finger in the baby's mouth, and the little thing sucked greedily. "I need a cotton bandage, Charles, and a medicine bottle," said Millie.

Millie half-filled the bottle with milk, twisted the cotton bandage, and pushed it into the milk as if it were the wick to an oil lamp. Then, holding the bottle with her fingers, she put the cotton to the baby's lips. Milk trickled along the tiny girl's cheeks and completely coated Millie's arm, but the baby was getting at least as much on the inside as she was on the outside.

Tomas watched the proceedings until he was sure the baby was eating. Then he laid his hand on the tiny head for a moment before he turned and walked out.

"Tupac," Charles said, "we need you to go to the village. Find a woman who can be a wetnurse for the baby until Mia is found. We will pay her to care for the child."

Millie looked down at the tiny thing lying in her arms. *Of course, we need a wet nurse. I can't keep feeding you goat's milk from rags, can I? But even if someone else feeds you, I will take care of you, little one. I promise—until your mother is found.*

"Unnnn—" Otis sat up, putting a hand to his head. "Millie, I thought you had a . . . baby!"

"It's Mia's baby," Savannah explained.

"Remember when you were six, and I told you about the stork?" Charles asked, pulling Otis to his feet. "Well, you and I need to talk."

"Of course it's Mia's," Otis said. "It was just so sudden, and—and I wasn't expecting a baby."

"How's the leg?" Charles asked his friend.

"It's fine," Otis said.

Señorita Armijo wheeled Angela into the room. "I hear there is a baby—oh, the dear thing! Señorita, have blankets and nappies brought immediately! I put Savannah's things away in a trunk in her room. Bring them!" Millie explained about Mia once again, then sighed as Don Rael appeared. It was beginning to feel very crowded in the room. Millie wondered if he had ever seen the kitchen of his hacienda before.

"It is an Indian child," he said, moving his wife's chair away from Millie. "Do not become too attached to it. They are born and die every day. We will send it back to the village."

"For shame, Francisco." Angela lifted her eyes to him. "It is a baby girl! She will be welcome in our home."

"Then the mother must be found immediately. If we do not find her, every beggar child in the country will be arriving at my door. I will not allow it! We are not running an orphanage, Angela!"

"Of course, dear," Angela said. "The baby is going to need the bassinet from the old nursery. Señorita, have it brought to Millie's parlor."

"Since you have this under control, Don Rael," Charles said, "I believe that I will help Tomas look for the mother."

"Perhaps the girl has killed herself," Don Rael said, folding his arms. "What will you do then?"

"She hasn't," Millie said. "She ran away because she thought her baby was dead, but she took a blanket. If she were going to kill herself, she wouldn't have done that."

Charles had not said that Mia might need a doctor when she was found, but when he came back into the room to kiss Millie good-bye he was carrying his bag.

Lord, protect Mia, Millie prayed as Charles went out. *Protect Mia's life and bring her back to her daughter.*

Don Rael took his wife away and Tupac left to find a wet nurse. Savannah was dragged away by Señorita Armijo, leaving Consuela and Rosarita to worry over Millie and the baby.

"I feel completely useless," Otis said, glaring at his crutch as if he wished he could hurl it across the room. "What can I do?"

"Pray," Millie said. "You can pray."

The storm, which seemed to have crawled up to the mountaintop and waited, came leaping down the slopes again, rolling over the hacienda and the village. Somewhere, a frightened, brokenhearted girl was out in the storm while Charles and Tomas looked for her.

Millie sat by the stove and held the baby close while Consuela and Rosarita watched her and whispered, shaking their heads. It was over an hour before Señorita Armijo returned with baby clothing, soft and smelling of the cedar chips that had been tucked in with them to keep the moths out. It was clear the Señorita did not think that the clothes should be worn by a pauper child. Millie thanked her anyway before she tied a diaper on the baby, then she chose a baby gown of softest wool, the hem rich with seed pearls and gold thread.

"There," Millie cooed when the baby was dressed. "A perfect little princess skin to dress a baby bunting in. You are the finest baby in all of Bolivia, I'm sure."

It was past ten when Tupac blew in out of the night, but he had no wet nurse with him.

"I asked every mother of a baby," he said. "No one will take this child."

"No one?" Millie asked in dismay.

"They said she belongs to Wanunu."

"That hideous woman is not coming near her!" Millie held the baby closer.

Tupac spread his hands. "Wanunu says the baby is hers. She says that you were cooking it, and that you have been feeding babies to the people to make them into Christians."

"That is the most ridiculous thing — where would I have gotten those babies?"

Tupac shrugged and spread his hands again in a plea. "Tupac," Millie said, "I know that it is cold and stormy and horrid outside. But I will need more goat's milk for her next feeding." He picked up the bucket and disappeared out the door.

By the second feeding Millie was becoming more adept at the procedure, rolling the wick tight, making it fit in the neck of the bottle, and holding it with one finger so the baby could not swallow it. Still, she tucked a kitchen towel around the child to keep the excess milk off the fine new clothes. When she was full, Millie carried her to the parlor, and sat up in the chair they had moved close to the stove for Otis. The bassinet had been placed in the room just as Angela instructed, but Millie did not want to leave her alone. The little one's skin was red and wrinkled because she had been born too soon, and after her ragged start in life, Millie was afraid a chill would carry her away.

When Charles came back in the gray light of dawn, Millie was still sitting in the chair, the baby in her arms. "We haven't found her," he said, looking exhausted. "The storm blew away any trace or tracks that she might have left. Tomas is still looking. How is this little one doing?"

"She has a good appetite for goat's milk," Millie said, smiling as he touched the baby's cheek. "And that's good, as no one will nurse her." She explained what Tupac had told her about the village women.

"Give them a few days," Charles said. "They will realize how ridiculous that is." Millie put the baby down long enough to tuck Charles into bed with a kiss, then went back to sit with her.

"What are you going to name her?" Otis said when he came out of his room hours later.

"I'm not going to name her," Millie said. "Mia will do that when Tomas brings her back."

But Tomas did not come back that day, and Millie kept Tupac busy bringing goat's milk. The baby woke every two hours, squirming and mewing for food. By nightfall, Millie was exhausted.

"I don't think you will be able to keep this up very long," Charles said. "We may have to find a village woman to help."

"None of them will. Even Consuela and Rosarita have been hesitant to speak to me today. And they know I do not cook babies!" Millie was so tired that she felt like crying.

"Ahem," Otis said, flushing quite pink. "I . . . I could help."

"I had no idea you knew anything about babies," Charles said.

"Well . . . " He loosened his collar. "I don't. But I've had kittens and such. How different can this be? If Millie could feed her until midnight each night I could feed her until dawn. Just until Mia returns, of course."

Millie showed Otis how to feed and burp the baby, and gave strict instructions about not walking about with her, or leaving her in a draft.

"Where could Mia have gone?" Millie asked when she collapsed at last into the bed.

More Threats

"Up the mountain, or over the pass, back to Yungas," Charles said. "Wherever she is, I pray God keeps her safe." He shook his head.

Millie prayed herself to sleep that night, and all night in her dreams Mia was calling from somewhere dark and lonely, but Millie could not find her. She was glad when she woke to the sunlight at last.

Otis was reclining in his chair, his foot up on a rest, his Bible open in one hand, the other holding the sleeping baby to his chest. He sighed deeply as Millie took the baby from his arms. "Now, Ella, don't cry," he said. "Millie will take good care of you."

"Ella?" Millie repeated.

"It's not a name, really," he said, standing up. "It's just something to call her . . . until her mother returns, you know."

⌒

But her mother didn't return. When Tomas came down the mountain three days later, he had found no sign of Mia. Millie decided that she would go into Orofino herself and find a woman to help care for the child. She made a pot of stew to take with her, and Tupac trotted at her side. Millie smiled at each person she met, but they did not smile in return. Not one woman took her arms, or offered her a kiss. They turned their eyes away or looked in horror at the soup pot she carried, making signs to ward off evil.

Millie sighed when a familiar face appeared. "There's Julio, Tupac," Millie said. "Tell him we have good, hot food for anyone who is hungry or ill." Julio was playing a stone-tossing game with six of his friends.

Millie's Fiery Trial

Tupac called out to him, but the boy backed away from them, shaking his head. Tupac waved his fingers, palm down, beckoning his friend as Millie had seen parents call a child, but Julio raised his hand, palm outward like a policeman ordering them to stop, and shook it back and forth. *No.* Millie did not need her few words of Quechua to understand what he meant. Julio's friends began to gather round, staring at Millie. One of the larger boys laughed, pointing at the soup pot, then at Julio's belly. *They are telling him he ate the baby*, Millie realized.

Suddenly, Julio stooped and picked up a stone. He threw it hard, and it caught Millie on the shoulder. Before she could react, the other children reached for stones as well.

"Philistines!" Tupac bellowed, and charged into the group. He caught Julio in the belly with his shoulder, and they tumbled to the ground, fists flying. Boys danced around them, cheering them on. Millie set down the soup and waded into the mob, still blinking back tears from the hurt in her shoulder. Grabbing a collar with each hand she pried them apart, barely resisting the urge to shake them.

Chaska appeared and called urgently to her son. Millie released him, and all of the children ran after him, looking over their shoulders as if she were a dangerous threat. Someone had tipped over the soup, and a skinny dog was lapping it from the dirt. Tupac wiped blood from his nose.

"They are not Philistines," Millie said, cleaning the rest of his battered face with the corner of her apron. "They are your friends, and they do not understand."

"They understand this," Tupac said, holding up his fist. "Pretty good, eh? Like Samson!"

Millie sighed. "Help me find the lid to the kettle, and remind me to speak to Otis regarding his story selections."

"I don't think you should go into town alone anymore," Charles said as he put a compress on her bruise.

"They were just children throwing stones." Millie winced.

"Stay home at least for a few days, until this blows over," Charles replied firmly.

"I suppose you are right. No one will eat my cooking anyway."

But it did not blow over, not in a week or a month. And Mia did not return. Ella grew fat and happy, cooing at Charles or Otis, and following Millie everywhere with her eyes.

"It is ridiculous," Millie said after Bible study one morning. "Wanunu has destroyed all of the progress I had made, all of the friendships. It wasn't even some dark magic that did it—it was simply trickery and lies!"

"It seems to me that lies have destroyed quite a lot in this old world," Otis said. "After all, Satan didn't storm Eden with demons, or terrorize Adam and Eve with unnatural happenings. He just made them believe a lie. If it worked so well before, why not use it again?"

"You can be very troubling when you are profound," Charles said to his friend. "Did you know that? We will just keep praying and showing God's love. They will come around."

But as the weeks passed, Millie did not see a change. She was shunned by the women each time she went into town. Even Consuela and Rosarita seemed hesitant, almost afraid of the infant.

"Because she has no soul," Savannah explained.

"Pish-tosh," Millie said. "She has a beautiful soul, created by God, her Heavenly Father."

Don Rael pretended the child did not exist, neither complaining nor asking about her—partly, Millie was sure, because of the change that had come over Angela. It was clear that she was not only improving, but that the consumption had given up its hold on her completely. Charles thought it was due more to prayer and the fresh air in the garden than anything he had done. Though she was still weak, she walked in the garden now, holding Millie's arm, rather than being pushed in her chair.

"I have decided to hold a ball," she said as they walked in the garden one day.

"The kind you had at home, Mother? In Georgia?" Savannah asked. The little girl was often with her mother now, eager to hold the hand she had not been allowed to touch for so long.

"Yes," Angela said. "Just like that."

"But who will you invite?" Millie asked. Aside from a few Dons who had come to discuss business with Don Rael, she had seen almost no company at the hacienda.

"That is not a problem," Angela said with a laugh. "Before I became ill we hosted the most marvelous parties. People would travel up from La Paz and come over the mountains. They would stay a week or more, of course. Bolivians love a fiesta, and we will have fiesta for a week!"

"And dancing," Savannah reminded her.

"Yes, dancing. If—" Angela looked to Millie. "If our pianist can be persuaded to play a waltz or two."

"Possibly even a cotillion and a polka," Millie smiled. "But only if Savannah is allowed to dance."

"Of course! We shall start lessons immediately. It takes months to plan such a party. I'm going to need a new dress. I haven't had a new dress in —" Suddenly her eyes welled up. "Millie," she said. "Did you know that God is good?"

"Very good," Millie agreed, linking arms with her. The three walked back to the house, where Otis was watching Ella.

"Otis," Angela teased, taking the child from his arms, "I don't think there has ever been a stranger nursery maid."

"Otis has saved me from a great deal of lost sleep, and complete exhaustion," Millie said in her friend's defense. "No one is better with Ella."

"No one but her mother," Angela said, handing the baby to Millie. "Don't look so surprised, my dear. A child needs a mother. After all, who is going to take care of her if you don't? I have heard that affections for foundlings can be just as strong as for a child of your own. When I see you with little Ella, I believe it."

"Charles," Millie said that night, as she played with the baby's dark curls, "I do believe that Mia will come back one day. But if she does not . . . "

"Then little Ella will be Ella Landreth," he said, stooping to kiss the baby's cheek. "Jesus adopted us, after all. How could we do less for a little one of His?"

It was only days later that Charles's swelling returned in his hands and his feet and all the way up to his knees. He lay in bed with fever for eight days, and the weakness lasted a fortnight more. Millie and Otis prayed over him morning and evening, splitting their time between caring for Ella and caring for Charles.

Señor Torrez stopped Millie in the hall one day, catching her arm as she hurried past with a bowl of soup for her husband. She stopped so quickly that the soup almost spilled.

"My grandmother has a message for you," he said. "She has a claim on that child."

"She does not," Millie said, pulling her arm away. "Ella is in no part Wanunu's. Was that her whole message?"

"No," Señor Torrez seemed hesitant to go on.

"Well? Charles's soup is getting cold."

"Give her the baby, and your husband will live," he said evenly.

"I have a message for her," Millie said. "She will never lay hands on Mia's child."

"She will not harm it." Señor Torrez spread his hands as Tupac did when he was making a plea. "It should have been her great-grandchild, after all. Romoldo was to have married her granddaughter, Simeona, yes? And you, Señora Landreth, do not know our customs. You cannot raise the baby in the old ways."

"In lies and deceit?" Millie pulled her arm away. "Certainly not! Charles's and Ella's lives are in Jesus' hands, Señor Torrez. Not those of Wanunu."

When he was able to walk around again, there was a stiffness in Charles's gait, his shirts hung baggy on his shoulders, and he shuffled like an old man, hardly lifting his feet.

"Have you any idea what is causing your illness?" Millie asked.

"I do not," he said, "nor how to treat it."

"Well, you will be back to the clinic in no time. You are not to worry about your patients missing you, either."

"No one is coming to the clinic," Charles said. "Not one person has come since Mia disappeared."

"Charles! Why didn't you say something?" Millie exclaimed.

"You have been very busy with the baby," he said. "And Tomas and I have had more time to work on language lessons. Will you send for him, Millie? I have the whole sermon translated, but I still make mistakes in pronunciation. I can work on that, at least."

Tomas came to their rooms daily after that, helping Charles with his pronunciation while Charles scribbled notes to himself. Tomas was picking up almost as much English as Charles was Quechua. He had a fine mind, and great curiosity about the world outside of Orofino. It was almost comical to listen as they discussed the Bible, religion, or politics in a mishmash language of their own. Millie was not sure who was more frustrated when their attempts at discussion failed. Charles would brood over a cup of tea, while Tomas wrung his hands and paced. Once in a while, Millie would catch Tomas gazing at Ella with a sad, faraway look in his eye, and her heart hurt for him, and for Mia as well, wherever she was.

Millie did not tell Charles about her talk with Señor Torrez until he was on his feet again.

"Ridiculous," he said. "This illness has nothing to do with Wanunu. I had symptoms before we ever met her. I just did not want to tell you. But Millie, I want you to know that even if I were dying, I would never give up Ella to her."

Weeks blurred together for Millie, as Charles seemed just on the point of recovery, only to be struck down again. Wave after wave of fever passed through him, devouring his flesh, and stealing the youth from his eyes.

It was mid-October and spring had tinged the dry hills green before Charles was up and walking again. He made his slow way about the hills behind the hacienda, Tomas one step behind him, watching out lest he stumble.

Millie watched as he practiced his sermon on the hill, a scarecrow of a man with only Tomas and two sheep as an audience.

Lord, what a spectacle we have become, she prayed. *A bruja who cooks babies and feeds them to people, a child without a soul, and a medicine man who preaches to sheep and tola shrubs. It is no wonder that the people of Orofino will not listen to us. Isn't it about time for the flaming chariots to arrive?*

"Otis," Charles said that evening, as the early summer wind blew in the open window, "what was that Scripture you gave me last week?"

Ella was sitting on Millie's lap, reaching for everything in sight, and giggling with delight when her adopted mother took it away.

" 'In all my prayers for all of you, I always pray with joy because of your partnership in the gospel from the first day until now, being confident of this, that he who began a good work in you will carry it on to completion until the day of Christ Jesus.' That's Philippians chapter 1, verses 4 through 6," Otis said.

"That's right," Charles said. "Did He start a work here? Were we really called to Bolivia?"

"Of course," Millie said. "Don't you remember your dream? Tomas—"

"Tomas has listened to me talk about Jesus every day for months. He listens as I preach to the rocks and tola shrubs, because no one else will listen. And he still has not accepted the Lord. No one has. We have been here almost a year, and not one soul has been saved. Not one."

More Threats

"Ella was saved," Millie said. "She would be dead if we had not come, and she will be raised in a Christian home and taught about Jesus."

"That's true," he said. "Jesus would have come to Bolivia to save just one person. He would have died for that." The baby smiled and reached up to him, but Charles was not strong enough to lift her. "Not now, sweetheart," he said. "Pappa needs to sleep."

"Otis," Millie said when he left the room, "I'm afraid. Perhaps we should think of going back. Charles should see a doctor."

Otis shook his head. "He won't go, Millie. Don't you remember when Fan died? You talked about God giving us one life to spend. Charles is spending his for the people here in Orofino."

Lord, Millie prayed, *my husband is dying before my very eyes! I know You've sent us here, but it seems nothing good has been gained. You gave us one life to spend, but are we to spend it here — battling sickness and threats and all of this darkness?*

CHAPTER

12

A Big Request

*And without faith it is impossible
to please God, because anyone
who comes to him must believe
that he exists and that he
rewards those who earnestly
seek him.*

HEBREWS 11:6

A Big Request

herefore put on the full armor of God, so that when the day of evil comes, you may be able to stand your ground, and after you have done everything, to stand,' " Millie read out loud. *How long, Lord? How long must we stand before we see Your hand in this? How long until these trials come to an end?*

Millie closed her Bible and rested her head on Charles's shoulder. They were seated on the garden bench she had once shared with Angela. Tonight Angela would waltz at the grandest party the Hacienda de Rael had seen in years, and Charles was the invalid who was confined by the garden walls.

As hard as it was to watch his body grow more frail, it was harder still to see the sparkle gone from his eyes. *I know that faith is being sure of what we hope for, and certain of what we do not see, Jesus. But Your Word says that hope deferred makes the heart sick, but longing fulfilled is a tree of life. Don't let Charles's heart grow sick, Lord. I want to hear him joke again. I want to hear him laugh. You healed Angela, Lord. I know You can heal Charles. I just don't understand why . . .*

"Dr. Landreth?" Millie sat up as Don Rael bowed. "Do you mind if I sit with you?"

"Not at all," Charles said, and Don Rael took the other bench.

"I have come to talk to you about a very serious matter. I made up my mind to speak to you some time ago, but there has never been a good time. My wife has asked Señora Landreth to play waltzes at the party tonight. If I wait until after the party, you may think I have abused my position as a host by asking for this, considering what I have to say . . . "

He stood and started pacing, his hands folded behind his back. "I am thankful for everything you have done for my wife, and for the clinic you built." He did not mention that the clinic served no patients. "There is no easy way to say this." He stopped and faced them. "I do not want your death on my hands. I have been thinking of this for some time, as I said, but did not mention it, as it was not the season for travel. Bolivia does not agree with you. I am afraid, for your own good, that I must end our agreement."

Charles seemed to collapse into himself, and Don Rael looked away as he continued. "I have arranged for your travel next month. A wagon will take you to the coast. I do not believe you should wait any longer. If you do, you may be too weak to travel."

Hope and confusion sprang up together in Millie's mind. *We're going home! I can take Charles to a doctor! But oh, we have failed. God sent us, but we failed.*

Charles took a breath, and let it out slowly. "About the clinic," he said. "You have a young man in Orofino who would make an excellent doctor. He has served as my assistant, and if I could choose someone to take my place . . . "

"Does he speak Español?"

"No," Charles said. "He speaks Quechua and a little English."

Don Rael looked to the treetops and pursed his lips. "Stiff-necked peasants who will not learn the language of the educated! He cannot go to the university if he does not speak Español. If he is willing to learn, I will send him to school."

"Thank you," Charles said.

Don Rael stood up. "You are a good man, Señor Landreth. You live what you believe. I know you both are disappointed, but I hope that disappointment will not keep

you away from dinner tonight. Angela has invited guests. But I will understand if you do not want to play the piano for us, Señora Landreth."

"Of course, I will play," Millie said. "You have been most gracious to us, Don Rael."

"No one is good but God," Charles said when Don Rael had gone. "Millie, I believe I have failed Him."

"No, you haven't," Millie said, but Charles's steps were slower as they returned to the house.

"Leaving?" Otis grew pale when they gave him the news. "Arrangements have already been made? But God is not done with us here yet. I'm sure of it!"

"I'd better rest," Charles said. "I won't be able to sit through the party tonight."

"Otis, would you look after Ella for me this afternoon?" Millie asked. "I'd like to walk and talk to Jesus."

"Of course," Otis said.

Millie took her Bible and her walking shoes, leaving Ella perfectly content with her Uncle Otis, and Charles stretched across the bed with his arm over his eyes. *Don't let anyone see me leave,* she prayed as she walked down the hall. Guests had been arriving for days, and every room at the hacienda was prepared for company, with most of them full. Guests were still arriving, and Angela seemed to delight in the fact that the hacienda had rooms for them all. Most of the company did not speak English, and Millie had learned enough Spanish to hold a polite conversation about the weather or roast pork, but most of the ladies spoke too quickly for her to follow their conversations. Just now Millie did not feel like smiling and nodding, hoping someone would ask about pork so she could join the conversation.

Millie's Fiery Trial

Don Rael was standing with a group of men in the dining room as she crept past. Millie recognized the words "blasting powder" and tiptoed more quickly. If Don Rael could convince them to leave the ladies, Millie was sure he would have them all out at the mine blowing things to bits. She slipped out the door and took a deep breath of air. The air was always too thin, and as much as she tried, she never seem to get enough of it to satisfy her hungry lungs.

The path she chose wound its way up over the terraced hillside above the village. Millie had walked for half an hour before she stopped to catch her breath, looking out over the patchwork land. Whole families worked together in the fields below, planting or digging trenches that would direct the rainwater to the thirsty crops of potatoes, beans, and grain.

"These are the people You sent us to reach, Jesus," Millie prayed aloud. "Your treasures hidden in darkness. We haven't done too well, I'm afraid. The darkness is thick in this land, and our lamps seem to be sputtering."

"You should chew the coca leaf." Millie jumped at the words. "That would give you energy."

"And green teeth, Tupac. I thought you were playing with Savannah," Millie said.

"Señorita Armijo told her that you are going away soon. She says you are going back where you belong."

"It is true that we are going away," Millie said. "But right now, we belong here, where Jesus sent us."

"Tell me again how you know," Tupac said.

"If you come with me, I will tell you while we walk."

"You come with me," Tupac said. "I know a trail that is not too hard for you. You never have enough air for walking."

"Thank you," Millie said. Tupac led the way along what could only have been a goat path. Millie tried hard to have enough air to walk and talk at the same time, as she told him once again of Charles's dream, of seeing Tomas calling out to them. Tupac had heard it at least a dozen times in the past six months, but always listened very carefully, as if he expected it might change.

"He came here to help Tomas," Tupac said.

"And you, too, Tupac, and the people of Orofino. He came to tell them about Jesus."

"But Tomas was in his dream. Does Doctor Charles want to go?" Tupac was walking more slowly so that she could keep up.

"No," Millie said, "he wants to stay. But he is very ill, and Don Rael thinks it is best to send us home."

"Are you giving Mia's baby to Wanunu when you go?" Tupac asked.

"Never!" Millie said. "Why would you think such a thing?"

"Then Doctor Charles will die anyway. Tomas says that Wanunu sends the fevers, and the next time they come, Doctor Charles will die."

"That is not true!" Millie said firmly. "Charles belongs to Jesus. Jesus governs his life, not Wanunu. And Charles would never give the baby to Wanunu."

They came around a boulder, and the ground dropped away suddenly into the dark maw of an abandoned mine. A hideous jackal face was carved into the stone above the opening to the mine. The statue head was decorated with ribbons, their colors long faded, and flags were tied to the stones around it. An empty liquor bottle, the contents of which had apparently been poured into the stone creature's mouth, still lay beneath it.

"What is this?" Millie asked.

"Tio Sopay," Tupac said, watching her closely.

"Oh, yes, Charles told me about Tio Sopay." She sat down on a rock. "He said that there is a face of Tio Sopay outside the mine that he visited. Why is there a whisky bottle?"

He shrugged. "The miners give cigars and whisky to Tio Sopay before they go underground. Tio Sopay owns all the silver of the earth. We give him gifts so that he will let us take his wealth."

Millie picked up a small stone and tossed it at the stone face. It bounced off the snarling snout. Tupac caught his breath.

"You must not do that, Millie," he said. "Tio Sopay is very powerful. The mountains themselves rest on him, and their roots go into him."

"Do you believe that?" Millie asked, picking up another stone. Tupac took it from her hand. "He does not own the silver or the gold or the jewels from the ground. The mountains do not rest on him. Those are lies," Millie said.

"I have felt his power," Tupac said. "Wanunu calls his creatures from the earth to bring sickness."

"I agree, he does have power," Millie said, "but not as much as he would like." She took her Bible out of her knapsack. "Do you know what this is?"

"It's your book," Tupac said. "The book Otis finds stories in." He made a muscle. "Samson! And David who threw rocks."

"This is the most important book in the world," Millie said, "because it tells us the truth about God."

"Otis said that too," Tupac replied.

"And it tells us the truth about Tio Sopay. It says he is a liar and a murderer. Tio Sopay has many names in the

Bible, Tupac. He is called a dragon and a serpent, Tio Sopay and Satan."

"Otis never told us Tio Sopay was in the book."

"Listen." Millie opened her Bible to Ezekiel 28:12 and began to read: " 'You were the model of perfection, full of wisdom and perfect in beauty. You were in Eden, the garden of God; every precious stone adorned you: ruby, topaz and emerald, chrysolite, onyx and jasper, sapphire, turquoise and beryl.' "

"That cannot be Tio Sopay in God's garden," Tupac said. "Tio Sopay is not full of wisdom and beauty."

"He was when God made him," Millie said before she continued. " 'You were anointed as a guardian cherub, for so I ordained you. You were on the holy mount of God; you walked among the fiery stones. You were blameless in your ways from the day you were created till wickedness was found in you.' "

"That could be Tio Sopay," Tupac nodded. "He is full of wickedness."

" 'So I drove you in disgrace from the mount of God, and I expelled you, O guardian cherub, from among the fiery stones. Your heart became proud on account of your beauty, and you corrupted your wisdom because of your splendor. So I threw you to the earth.' "

Tupac put his hand on Millie's shoulder, stopping her. "God threw Tio Sopay down?" he searched her eyes. "It is in the book?"

"Yes, God allowed one of His Mighty Warriors to fight with Satan." She turned quickly to Revelation 12:7 and read: " 'There was war in heaven. Michael and his angels fought against the dragon, and the dragon and his angels fought back. But he was not strong enough, and they lost

their place in heaven. The great dragon was hurled down —
that ancient serpent called the devil, or Satan, who leads
the whole world astray.' "

"How? Is that in the book as well?" he asked.

"It's all in the book," Millie laughed. "God created people to be His children, and He put them in a garden where
He could walk and talk with them. But Satan, who lives as
Tio Sopay here, hated them. He wanted to destroy them
and hurt God. This is what the book says."

Millie turned quickly to Genesis 3 and quoted the passage.

" 'Now the serpent was more crafty than any of the wild
animals the Lord God had made. He said to the woman,
"Did God really say, 'You must not eat from any tree in the
garden'?"

" 'The woman said to the serpent, "We may eat fruit from
the trees in the garden, but God did say, 'You must not eat
fruit from the tree that is in the middle of the garden, and
you must not touch it, or you will die.' "

" ' "You will not surely die," the serpent said to the
woman. "For God knows that when you eat of it your eyes
will be opened, and you will be like God, knowing good
and evil." ' "

Tupac was concentrating very hard on the Bible in
Millie's hands.

"It was a lie, Tupac. The serpent lied about God, about
His heart for His children. And when His children believed
that lie, the world tumbled into darkness. Sin and sickness
and death came. Satan, or Tio Sopay, set himself up as a
god, and the evil angels who came with him as well, forcing
men and women to serve them as slaves. God could not
bear to see His children as slaves to Satan and death so He

came to destroy the works of Satan. He came to set His people free through the death and resurrection of His Son Jesus."

"Is this why Tomas needs help?" he asked.

"Yes," Millie said, feeling a spark of hope. "Unless you give your heart to Jesus, unless you make Him your King instead of Tio Sopay, then you are just a slave. You have been tricked."

Tupac considered the stone face above the mine. "I know that Tio Sopay is real," he said at last. "He has power. He can kill, if we do not do what Wanunu says. He killed my sister and made me ill. He is killing Doctor Charles."

"He has power," Millie agreed, "and he does many evil things on this earth. But his power is not greater than the power of Jesus. Those who belong to Jesus, like Charles, are under God's protection. Tio Sopay cannot kill them. They fight against Tio Sopay, and when they die, they will be with Jesus."

"What happens to those who do not fight against Tio Sopay?" Tupac asked.

"Tio Sopay takes them," Millie said, "into the darkness — spiritual darkness. But listen to what God's Book says: 'Now have come the salvation and the power and the kingdom of our God, and the authority of his Christ.' In God's Book Jesus said, 'Now is the time for judgment on this world; now the prince of this world will be driven out.' Jesus threw Tio Sopay out of Heaven and defeated him on earth, and anyone who wishes can be free."

"Tomas is a stubborn man," Tupac said. "When I ask him about God Jesus, he says, 'Wait, wait and see what happens.' But we do not have time to wait. If this is true, how will the Quechua know it when you go away? Who will tell them?" Tupac took a deep, shuddering breath. "I must know if it is true."

He stood looking at the statue of Tio Sopay for a full minute, then abruptly turned his back to it and spread his arms, looking wide-eyed into the heavens. "God of Señora Landreth," he shouted, "I am Tupac. You saved me from the fever in the night. Do you remember? I want to know if You are the One God like Your Book says. I'm going to ask you to do something." Chills were running up and down Millie's spine. "If You are the mighty God, the One who made everything, then . . . send me a Bible book. I will learn to read it." Millie realized that she had sucked in her breath. Tupac was not finished. "Send one for Tomas as well, and one for Mia and one for Savannah . . ."

Millie bit her lip. Was he going to ask for a whole printing press? In the year they had been in Bolivia they had been unable to find even one Bible for Otis.

"If You are the great God, send them tonight. I will talk to Tomas and tell him You will do this." Millie closed her eyes. "And if You do this," Tupac said, "I will come into Your kingdom. My blood will be Your blood, my bones Your bones, my breath Your breath. Because You fought for me, I will fight for You all of my life."

Lord, Millie prayed as they went down the mountain, *I know I am supposed to have faith. But there is not one available Bible in all of Bolivia.*

CHAPTER

13

Amazing
Encounters

*Your people will rebuild the ancient
ruins and will raise up the age-old
foundations; you will be called
Repairer of Broken Walls,
Restorer of Streets with
Dwellings.*

ISAIAH 58:12

illie hurried to her room. "Charles?" He was not on the bed. She removed her bonnet and sank to her knees. *Lord*, she prayed, *show me what to do. Should I give Tupac my Bible? But even if I give him both mine and Charles's, we will still be two Bibles short! Lord, we have been working so long for this, and now there is nothing I can do!*

"Home at last?" Charles came into the room, adjusting the cravat at his neck. "It's a good thing Otis was here to tie this thing . . . Are you all right?" He shrugged self-consciously. "I know the jacket no longer fits, but surely I don't look pitiful enough to drive you to your knees."

"It's not that," Millie said, standing quickly. "Tupac has prayed . . . he has almost prayed to accept the Lord."

"He prayed? That's wonderful!"

"It's not wonderful, Charles. He asked for something impossible," Millie said.

"Slow down," Charles said. "Tell me exactly what happened."

Millie explained her discussion with Tupac on the mountain. "He asked for Bibles," she said at last. "Lots of Bibles."

"Bibles," Charles repeated.

"Yes, and we don't have any," Millie said.

"That is certainly true. Dearest, are you going to the party in your garden dress?"

"Good heavens!" Millie looked at the clock. "I don't have time—"

"Of course you do," Charles said. "We will simply be fashionably late. It's not as if they will start the waltzing without you."

Charles waited with Otis while Millie changed as quickly as possible into the blue satin gown she had set out for the party. It was the first time she'd had occasion to wear such finery in all the months since their arrival. There was no time to press curls into her hair or arrange it in any elegance at all.

"Bibles?" Otis asked when she made her appearance, plainer than she had intended, but not too horribly late. "How many?" he asked.

"Four," Millie said, taking Charles's arm. "At least four. But he didn't specify the language they should be printed in."

"That makes it easier, don't you think?" Otis said.

Millie felt as if she were in the presence of madmen. "Otis! We have been praying for Bibles since we arrived in Bolivia, and we have none. What are we going to do?"

"Señora Landreth." Señorita Armijo was at the door. She had agreed to sit with Ella, but not, Millie was sure, before Angela had spoken to her. She looked sourly at the baby sleeping in the bassinet.

"She shouldn't wake," Millie said. "Not until her midnight feeding, and we will be back before then."

"If she does wake," Otis said, "send for me."

"What are we going to do?" Millie asked again, as they walked down the hall.

"Millie, my love," Charles said, stopping just outside the conservatory door. "Being ill has taught me one thing. When there is nothing you can do, then you do nothing — nothing but pray."

"But Charles!" she exclaimed.

"If Jesus does not answer Tupac's prayer," Charles said gently, "we cannot. Now you are going to step inside and be

entertaining. Don Rael may be sending me home, for which I don't blame him a bit, but he has been a wonderful host. You have promised to play."

"I play while you pray," Millie said. "I see."

"Would you walk me to the couch before you begin?" asked Charles.

"Of course," Millie said. A group of men stood around the large fireplace at the far end of the conservatory, Angela just visible among them. They were finely dressed with braid and brocade, boots polished to a high sheen, coats and trousers tailored. The ladies wore gold tiaras or combs encrusted with diamonds, sapphires, or pearls, in their hair. There were even jewels on the dancing slippers that flashed beneath their petticoats. Millie was sure she had not seen such wealth at the grandest of the plantations in the South. Even Savannah wore a king's ransom, disguised as a tiara, on her small head, thinking no more of the riches than she would of play jewelry.

"Who is that?" Millie whispered, pointing with her chin to a man who stood apart from the group. He appeared to be young, twenty perhaps, and was dressed more simply than the others. He was clean and well kept, but he did not wear boots. He had on walking shoes instead, and they were worn at that.

"I don't know," Charles said. "He looks familiar, but I can't place him. Do you know him, Otis?"

"Ah! Dr. Landreth." Don Rael had seen them and motioned them over. "May I make introductions? Most of these gentlemen you have met." He waved at the Dons. "And this is Argus MacArgus. He is traveling through Bolivia, and we are fortunate enough to have him with us tonight."

MacArgus bowed, and Charles bowed in return. *He reminds me of Cyril and Don*, Millie thought, *all long legs and joints and bobbing Adam's apple.*

"I was just on my way to the couch," Charles said apologetically. "I'm afraid I cannot stand long these days." Millie took his arm and walked with him.

"Millie!" Angela moved to her side. "What a beautiful gown! But I should have sent jewels for you."

"Her eyes outshine sapphires," Charles said. "If you don't mind, ladies?" He lowered himself to the couch. "I am a little light-headed."

"May I steal your wife?" Angela asked. "I have been waiting forever for a dance, and I cannot wait any longer."

"Of course," Charles said.

"The Cremona Waltz," Angela announced as Millie sat down. They had gone over the play list endlessly, Angela asking if Millie could play this or that, searching for sheet music and lamenting the fact that they would not have an orchestra. She began to play, and Don Rael took his wife's hand. They danced the entire waltz together as their friends watched. The audience clapped, and Millie began to play the Pickwickian Quadrilles. Otis bowed to Savannah, who accepted the dance with a giggle and a curtsy, and other couples joined them on the floor. Millie played, moving from cotillions to waltzes and back again. Her own eyes were closed as she imagined dancing with Charles. *Will we ever dance again?* she wondered.

"I need a rest, I'm afraid," she said, standing up. Charles was no longer on the couch. Millie made her way through the crowd looking for him, but found MacArgus instead. "Have you seen my husband?" she asked.

"Charles, was it not? The fellow on the couch? He was not feeling well, and excused himself. He asked if you

would offer his apologies to the hostess, and said you were not to think of leaving the party. I think he went to have a talk with Jesus."

"You know Jesus?" Millie asked, surprised.

"Personally," the young man said, "and I'm very glad of it."

"I'm sorry to appear so surprised, but we have not met many in Bolivia who do."

"There are a few of us." His Adam's apple bobbed. "Here and there. You seem distressed, Mrs. Landreth. Might I help?"

"Not unless you have four Bibles in your pocket," Millie said.

"I do not," he said, "but—beg your pardon!" He had somehow managed to step backwards onto the hem of a señorita's dress. She flashed him a look that would have withered a bouquet and hurried away.

MacArgus started to scratch his head, then apparently realizing that would be considered improper, patted it instead. Millie took his arm, steered him out of the middle of the room, and stood him with his back safely against a wall.

"You were saying?" He looked bewildered. "Or was I saying? Ah! You have some difficulty?"

"Yes," Millie said. "You see, I was discussing the Bible with a young man today, and—"

"What subject?" His Adam's apple bobbed again. "I love the Bible."

"We were discussing Satan, actually," Millie said.

A look of disgust crossed his face. "Revelation 12:7, I hope. Michael and his angels fought against Satan." He cracked his knuckles, just as Cyril might have done when

discussing a recent bout of fisticuffs. "I love that Scripture." Suddenly he flushed, and put his hands behind his back. "I beg your pardon. Please go on."

"In fact," Millie could not help but laugh, "we did read that Scripture. I like it as well."

Otis appeared at Millie's elbow. "Where has Charles gone?" he asked.

"To our rooms," Millie said. "I think he wants some time alone with the Lord." The dinner bell rang, and Otis offered his arm.

"May I escort you, then?"

"Has Millie discovered your life story?" he asked MacArgus as they moved together in the line. MacArgus smiled.

"No, we were discussing Scripture."

"What brings you to Bolivia, Mr. MacArgus?" asked Millie.

"Call me Mac, please. I—"

"Pardon the interruption," Angela said. "I have taken the liberty of seating you all together at this end of the table. We will have dancing and dinner conversation in English. It's practically Heaven."

"Did you say you worked for Don Rael?" Millie asked as soon as they were seated.

"Oh, no, I work for—"

"Could you possibly speak a little louder?" Otis was seated opposite Millie, and he was leaning forward to hear.

"I was just about to say," the young man was practically shouting, "I work for God."

Angela lifted her eyebrows. "Then you are in good company! The Landreths work for God as well."

"What do you do for God?" Otis asked.

"I am currently a Bible agent, though before that —"

"A what?" Millie set her fork down.

"A Bible agent. I am carrying Bibles in my backpack throughout Bolivia and Peru. What I meant to say earlier, Mrs. Landreth, was that while I did not have four Bibles in my pocket, I do have seventeen in my backpack. Two are in English and . . . are you . . . crying?"

"I've just seen the answer to a prayer," Millie said. "One that we have been praying a very long time."

"Really?" Mac looked over his shoulder, as if expecting the answer to be standing behind him. "Oh! You mean the Bibles!"

"The boy I was discussing Scripture with," Millie explained. "He prayed today for the first time. He asked for God to give him a Bible tonight."

"Well!" Mac smacked his fist into his other palm. "We will take him one tonight!" He leaned forward, looking like a schoolboy suggesting that they sneak out of class. "How soon can we slip away?"

"Not until my dinner is finished, I hope," Angela said.

"Oh! Of course not. How rude of me, Señora. I wasn't thinking. How did you come to Bolivia, Mrs. Landreth?"

Millie explained about Charles's dream and coming to Bolivia, while Mac listened goggle-eyed. "God is . . . He is . . ." He touched his fingers to his temples. "I do not have the words to describe how wonderful He is!"

"I couldn't agree more," Millie said.

"I wish I could slip away with you," Angela said when dinner was done. "But I am afraid I must stay with the ladies. You will tell me all about it tomorrow, Millie?"

"Of course," Millie said, taking her friend's hand. "It has been a marvelous party, Angela."

Millie's Fiery Trial

Millie hurried to their rooms with the news. Señorita Armijo was nowhere to be seen. Charles was sitting up in the chair in his dressing gown. Either he had prayed himself to sleep, or he was petitioning God with his eyes closed and his mouth open.

"Charles, wake up," Millie said, stooping to kiss his cheek. "Argus has brought the Bibles. We are going down to deliver them now."

"Huh?" Charles rubbed the sleep from his eyes. Millie was almost too excited to make any sense at all, but when she finally did, Charles came wide awake.

"I'll just get ready, then," he said.

Millie's heart sank. *He could hardly walk to the end of the garden. How would he make it to town?* "Dearest," she said. "I don't think you need to change your clothes."

"She's right," Otis said as he and Mac arrived. "Why not make it a come-as-you-are affair? I can't wait any longer."

"That's not what I meant!" Millie said, but Charles was already putting on his shoes. Otis scooped the sleeping baby out of her bed and wrapped her in a blanket. While Millie put on her walking shoes, Argus showed Charlie the two Bibles he was carrying in his pockets.

"Shhhh!" Otis said.

Millie took the lantern and they slipped out down the long hallway to the front door and out into the darkness. Charles made it almost to the road before he stopped.

"Charles, dear, you need to go back," Millie said.

"Then he would miss the miracle," Mac said. He grabbed Charles's arms, put them over his shoulders, and lifted him onto his back. "Here we go, piggyback just like when you were a kid."

"I feel ridiculous," Charles said, as they started walking again.

"Ridiculous? I wouldn't say that," Mac puffed. "Cumbersome, perhaps. Boney, definitely. But not ridiculous."

"You have no idea how long we have been praying for Bibles," Charles said, apparently settling in for the ride. "It has been almost a year."

"Well, that's how long I've been on my way," Mac said. "So it's a good thing you prayed when you did. Could you shift a bit to the left? There . . . thank you."

"Tupac only prayed today," Millie pointed out. "He was answered immediately."

"God often answers before you even pray. Ooof! Don't think I am not happy to do this, but . . . is it much farther?"

"Just here," Millie said, stopping at the door.

"Halleluiah!" Mac lowered Charles to the ground. For the first time he seemed shy. "Could you give them the Bibles, Charles?" he whispered, taking them from his pockets. "They don't know me."

Charles took the Bibles as Millie rapped on the door. Tupac opened it, his eyes going from their faces to the Bibles. The boy's eyes widened. "Is it the Book?" Tupac asked.

"Yes," Millie said. "It is the Book."

Tupac fell to his knees, Tomas beside him. Charles began speaking to them in Quechua, explaining how to give their lives to the Lord. Mac stood behind Charles, grinning from ear to ear. When Tomas began to pray, Mac stepped back, almost out of the lamplight, bouncing on his heels and humming.

"Are you humming 'Bringing in the Sheaves'?" Millie whispered.

"Yes. Quite appropriate, don't you think?" he said.

"I do." Millie smiled, and then stepped closer to Charles so that she could hear what was said. Tupac got up from his knees and wrapped his arms around her waist.

"There's someone I'd like you to meet," Millie said. "He came a very long way to bring you a Bible. Mac?" He wasn't in the circle of light.

"Who are you calling?" Tupac asked.

"The young man who was with us when you opened the door," Millie said.

"There was no man with you," Tupac said. "Just Doctor Charles and the books."

"Of course there was," Millie said, looking both ways down the street. But there wasn't.

"Ella!" Otis's voice squeaked to the infant. "I think we've just walked with an angel!"

They laughed and talked until dawn in the poor dwelling of Tomas and Tupac. Then they ate parched grain and drank goat's milk, and Otis laughed some more when he realized it was like Communion.

"I think we had better get back to the hacienda," Charles said at last. "I am still in my pajamas!"

Tomas grabbed Charles's arms. "You must tell them," he said.

"My friend," Charles shook his head. "I believe it is you who must tell them. God sent us to help you, Tomas."

Tomas looked at him for a moment and then broke into a smile. "Then you must pray for me as I tell them. An angel carried you here," he said, "but I will carry you now."

The market was filling with people when they arrived, people unloading wagons, carts, and llamas, spreading rugs and stacking piles of potatoes, while the first customers walked about. They stopped to look at the spectacle of Tomas carrying the much-larger Charles on his back. Charles's toes practically touched the ground, but Tomas carried him with ease. Tupac found a bucket and turned it on end to make a seat for Charles. Millie stood beside him, her arm around his shoulders.

A crowd had already gathered by the time Tomas jumped onto an empty table, and when he began to speak, Millie put her hand over her mouth. She did not know the meaning of all of the words, but she had heard them before, many times. Tomas was preaching Charles's sermon, telling the town of Orofino about Jesus.

"There! That's the part I never could get right," Charles said. "Tomas would never tell me what I was saying. He would only laugh."

One by one, the people in the market stopped to listen. The crowd grew larger, and when Tomas finished, Millie had never seen the people so quiet or so still.

Suddenly a woman sobbed, and with the sound the heavens opened and the Truth came down on Orofino. Men and women cried out for forgiveness, pulling charms and magic items from their necks and wrists, and throwing them to the ground in front of Tomas, before sinking to their knees.

They were in the market for half the day, it seemed, praying for people before Tomas insisted that it was time for Charles to go home. "I believe he's right," Otis said. "It's not proper to wear pajamas past noon."

Charles insisted on walking as far as he could, but before they were halfway up the hill Tomas was carrying him again. They took the servant's path to the kitchen, to avoid being seen by the guests.

Consuela and Rosarita were waiting for them when they entered, full of questions. The man who brought the flour for the evening meal had told them that God Himself was walking through Orofino. When Tupac explained to them all that had happened, they gave him three meat pies.

The disappearance of Mac did not cause so much as a ripple in the overly full hacienda, where there had been so many comings and goings in the past week. Savannah, however, was very upset that she had been left out of the all-night heavenly affair. But when she found that she had seen the angel MacArgus and Tupac had not, she teased him about it until he threatened to take Weeker away.

CHAPTER

14

Turning Toward Home

*"I tell you the truth," Jesus replied, "no
one who has left home or brothers
or sisters or mother or father or
children or fields for me and
the gospel will fail to receive
a hundred times as much in
this present age."*

MARK 10:29–30

Turning Toward Home

he joy of seeing Tomas and Tupac come to the Lord, along with so many people of Orofino, was food and drink to Charles. He ate more, laughed more, and walked in the garden, praying for an hour each evening.

For the next week Tomas came to the hacienda and sat at the foot of his bed, listening to every word Charles said, and Charles, knowing their time in Bolivia was short, poured his heart and his soul into the teaching. He read from the Scriptures, then translated them into Quechua, looking to Tupac if he had difficulty with a word. Charles was laying the foundation of Christ, stone upon stone, in the young man's heart.

Otis was in the market again, teaching the children. Millie had given him a list of Bible stories she felt were appropriate. But when she saw three little boys with slings Otis had made for them busy slaying a field of boulders, she was sure he had not followed the list at all.

It seemed that prayer after prayer was now being answered, as much as there had been silence before. God was truly pushing back the darkness over the village through the light of the gospel! Millie set about packing with joy. While Charles's fevers did not disappear, he seemed stronger and certainly able to travel. It had been God's plan that they come to Bolivia, and just as surely Millie's heart was now turning toward home.

Even Angela seemed to have caught the joy, delighting in the fact that she had entertained an angel. Bibles had been left in Mac's room for Otis and Savannah, and Millie could only smile when she saw Angela in the garden, reading a Bible aloud to her daughter. Only Don Rael and Señorita Armijo seemed disgruntled and annoyed, and for the same reason. Señor Torrez had left the valley with his grandmother Wanunu. The people of Orofino would not tolerate the woman any longer.

A week before Charles, Millie, and Otis were to leave, Savannah was telling her father about Mac's sudden leaving once again at breakfast.

"It means nothing," he said, waving at the empty chair. "People disappear here frequently, it seems. Where will I find a segundo that knows my lands and my mines? There is none."

"Speaking of . . . people disappearing," Otis said. "I'm not going back with you, Charles."

"Otis!" Charles exclaimed.

"Tomas and Tupac are babies in the Lord, even more than I was a year ago. How can they lead a church? They need someone to teach them how to read. I can do that . . . and . . . well, I'm here."

"That's true," Charles said slowly. "Are you going to remain at the hacienda, then?"

"I'm not going to live with my uncle," he flushed. "I'm sorry, Aunt Angela, but I love the people here, and they live in the village. They can't come and go here, so I'm going to take a little house there where the children can come if they wish. There is a sturdy little house by the market."

"Wanunu's house!" Savannah said.

"Well—er, yes. It will need a little cleaning, but there are two rooms."

"I think you are right," Charles said. "I believe you should stay."

"I am?" Otis looked pleased. "I was so afraid you wouldn't think so, and I just kept worrying. After all, who would look after Ella if I left?" Millie's heart froze.

"Ella is coming with us!" Everyone was looking at her. "Isn't she, Charles?" He looked as stricken as she felt.

"You always said you were keeping her until Mia returned," Otis said, looking from one to the other. "What will Mia do when she comes back and her daughter is gone?"

"What if she does not come back?" Millie asked.

"Then I will raise her as my own daughter," Otis said.

"Excuse me," Millie fled from the table, down the corridors to the parlor where Rosarita was sitting by the bassinet. "I will take her now. Thank you," Millie said, as she reached for the baby.

"Si," Rosarita's smile faded as she saw Millie's face, and Rosarita left the room, looking back uncertainly at the door.

Charles found Millie rocking the baby, and held them both for a time without speaking. "Otis is right," he said at last. "Ella must wait for Mia."

Millie spent that night listening to the soft breathing of the little girl. *I can't leave her, Jesus. How can I? I promised to take care of her until her mother returned. But the trip to Pleasant Plains is long and could be very dangerous. Two months on a ship would be hard enough on Charles, let alone a baby. Here she is safe and well cared for.*

Jesus, Millie prayed in the darkness, *You put this little one in my arms. I give her back to You. Please help me give her back to You.*

Millie's Fiery Trial

Millie spent her remaining days in Orofino being dragged from house to house by the women of the town. Many had prepared meals for her, in penance, she was sure, for treating her so badly. She was served kita quwi at several homes, as well as other things that she did not dare to ask the nature of, all cooked over open dung fires and served with bare fingers. Millie accepted each dish graciously, and prayed furiously before each bite, and often after as well.

On her last trip to town she went to Mia's house, empty now, with even the thin blanket gone from the door. The wind had piled dust in the corners, but there were tracks on the floor and smudges on the dusty bed. Someone had come here to sit alone. Tomas, she was sure. She could almost hear the haunting music of his pipes. Millie sat in the stillness of the hovel, remembering the sweet spirit of the girl who had lived here and cried on lonely nights as Tomas cried now.

Holy Spirit, help me to pray for them as You prayed for me. Don't let my heart forget them, ever. Don't let me forget Bolivia. Millie prayed until the square of sunlight from the door had climbed up the wall, and the shadows in the corners had grown dark. She shivered as she pulled her shawl around her, but it was only the chill of evening. The darkness that had walked in Orofino was gone.

When the wagon was packed, it was brought to the front of the hacienda behind the cart, which would carry the Landreths to the city of La Paz. Don Rael and Angela stood on the steps to bid Millie and Charles good-bye, and the whole town seemed to be crowded into the courtyard.

Charles took little Ella in his arms and held her close. "May the Lord bless and protect you," he said. He kissed the baby tenderly on the cheek, and then handed her to Millie.

"Good-bye, darling," Millie said, kissing the soft curls.

"Don't worry, Millie," Savannah said. "We will take care of her. Tupac will teach her to jump like a goat. And I will teach her about Jesus, as Mother is teaching me."

"Thank you, Savannah," Millie said through her tears.

Charles shook Otis's hand. "I don't suppose I'll see you again before we get to Heaven," Otis said.

"No," said Charles. "This was the kind of trip a person only makes once in their lifetime. But I will see you again in Heaven, my friend."

Millie handed Otis the baby and climbed into the cart beside Charles. Children ran after them through the town and up the hills. When they reached the pass above the mine, Tupac stood atop a boulder, silhouetted against the blue sky. Tomas was standing in the road, a Bible in his hand. He pulled himself into the cart and hugged Charles, then jumped down again. They were still standing there when the mules went around the bend and the valley was lost from sight.

For the first few days Charles slept in the cart, propped up by pillows. It was all Millie could do to keep his blankets tucked in. She felt like a general, issuing orders to the drivers each time they stopped: boil the water for tea, prepare the food, pitch the tents. She was glad for the work, as it kept her mind off of Ella. But still her arms ached to hold the warm little body, and her ears longed to hear a giggle.

Millie's Fiery Trial

They rested for a week in La Paz, to allow Charles to gain strength for the rest of the journey, and then set out once again, over the mountains and down to the coast. There was a wait of two days in Arica, their last days in Bolivia, and then they boarded the ship. It was larger and much more comfortable than the one they had made the journey down on, with a private cabin and dining room.

Charles sat in a deck chair wrapped in a llama wool blanket as the sails caught the wind, and the mountains of Bolivia disappeared into the sea. "Good-bye," Charles said.

Millie's heart was so full of sadness and joy that she couldn't speak. *Good-bye, forever*, she thought. *We're going home.*

When they reached New York at last, as Charles rested for two weeks, Millie wrote ahead to Lansdale and to Pleasant Plains, and when their stage reached Lightcap's Station, the whole town of Pleasant Plains had turned out to greet them. Millie found herself in a hurricane of hugs and kisses.

Stuart and Marcia were a tiny bit grayer at the temples, and Marcia's hands were laced with wrinkles, but Millie thought they looked wonderful. She breathed in the smell of her mother and father as they hugged her. Ru was certainly a man now. Adah stood proudly beside Frank Osborne, with little Frank Too at her side. "Look, Millie." Her sister held up her hand, with a ring on her finger. Annis jumped up and down. "They're married," she said.

"What? Why, Annis, you are the only girl Mamma has left," Millie said.

Aunt Wealthy Stanhope had reached Pleasant Plains just the day before. She had hardly greeted Millie and Charles before her fingers went to the fine shawl Millie was wearing.

"What a marvelous texture," she said. "Sheds water, like wool, I imagine? Of course it does. Otherwise llamas would soak up rain like cotton balls, and squish when they walked."

Charles laughed at the image of sodden llamas sloshing over the hills, and Millie realized it was the first time she had heard him laugh since they left Bolivia.

Don and Cyril arrived late and somewhat dusty. "Did anyone ever tell you that you look just like angels?" Millie asked when they put her down.

The twins looked at each other and shrugged. "Mother told me I did once," Don said. Cyril cracked his knuckles.

"Angels?" Ru said, examining his younger brothers.

"I have a story to tell about angels," Millie said as she kissed him.

"We have a thousand stories to tell!" Charles laughed. "But we know them all. We want to know what has been happening here."

"Jasmine Mikolaus," Millie said, spotting a stunning young lady with flashing eyes and a brilliant smile. "Is that you?"

"Welcome home, Millie," she said. "We have missed you so much!"

"Millie Keith!" Mrs. Prior pushed her way through the crowd. "I told her she shouldn't go cavorting off to the ends of the earth!" she declared, though Millie could remember her saying no such thing. "Look what it's done to you! You're skinny as a wild chicken. Well, well, we'll have you full of food and fit as a fiddle in no time. You're home now, thank heavens!"

Millie's Fiery Trial

That evening at Keith Hill there was a great deal of laughter and talk, and many exclamations over the gifts the Landreths had brought from Bolivia: soft blankets and hats, the musical instruments made of reeds and armadillo shells. But as Charles described the Quechua people, Millie slipped quietly out the back door. She walked through the gloaming, breathing the Indiana air as rich as wine, to the graveyard by the church. "Fan Keith," the simple stone marker read. "Beloved Daughter." There were two smaller headstones beside her. Millie sank to her knees on the green grass. "Toast with no butter was not such a bad idea after all," Millie said. "Though I don't suppose even that would have prepared me for a guinea pig. You would have loved Bolivia, Fan. You would have loved being a missionary." *Fan walked into the valley of the shadow of death to save those who were perishing. She took two little souls with her to Heaven. I'm sure she held two little hands in her own as they walked toward You, Lord, so they would not feel so alone.*

Millie felt a hand on her shoulder and looked up to find Celestia Ann, a gentle smile on her face. "I was with her when she died, you know. I was in a cot on the other side of the room, too sick to move a muscle. The last thing she said was, 'What I want to know is . . . '" Millie laughed in spite of herself. She could hear Fan saying that.

"And then she smiled," Celestia Ann said. "I think Fan has her answers at last."

"I'm sure she does," Millie said, getting to her feet. "I'm proud of you, Fan," she said. "As a very dear friend said, I don't suppose I'll see you again before we get to Heaven, but I know I will see you there." Millie walked back up Keith Hill arm in arm with Celestia Ann.

A puddle of Heaven on earth. That's what Frank Osborne had called Keith Hill once and that's what it seemed to Millie now. Aside from Mrs. Prior, everyone said she had not changed at all. But then, they could not see the little girl–shaped hole in her heart.

Is this the way You felt, Jesus? Millie wrote in her prayer journal. *Going home to the Father You loved, but leaving those You loved behind? How You must miss us and long for us to be with You! I thank You for the children of Bolivia that will be with You because we went, and the little ones Fan brought to You as well. Father, I will pray every day for Your missionaries. Send them, Father, send them to their neighbors, and to faraway lands. Oh, let us bring them to You!* She stopped and listened. "What are you whistling, Cyril?"

Cyril looked up from his whittling. "Bringing in the Sheaves," he said. "God sometimes just puts a song in my heart, and it has to come out. That's the song in my heart today."

"Mine too," Millie said, and went to look after Charles.

Charles spent the first month on the couch, looking out the same window that Millie had the year before she traveled to Roselands. He was not as fascinated with the small creatures as she had been. Instead, he perused medical journals and waited for the evenings, which were spent discussing pharmaceutical practices and new medications with Ru, or Scripture verses with Stuart.

Dr. Chetwood came once a week to check on him. At the end of four weeks, Dr. Chetwood stopped as he was putting on his top hat and gloves. "I can hardly approve of your recent practice," he said, "but I hate to see a keen mind wasted. Do you remember the offer I made before you foolishly left for South America?"

"I do," Charles said quietly. "You offered to leave me your practice."

"That was the one." Dr. Chetwood tapped his hat to adjust the fit. "Fortunately for you, I am still in moderately good health and can wait. But I could use a doctor who would stay at the office, handling the place while I am away on calls."

"I would be delighted," Charles said.

"Good," Dr. Chetwood said. "I will see you on Monday, then."

"Monday," Charles agreed, and Millie thought he looked happier than he had in months. That same Monday brought a packet of mail, among it a letter from Otis Lochneer.

"Here's news," Charles said, handing the letter to Millie.

God is so good. A child of His has come home. I had to tell you—I wish I could shout it loudly enough for you to hear, Millie. A young woman came to the clinic yesterday, a young woman with sad golden eyes. I thought she looked familiar, but I wasn't sure until she saw Ella, and I saw the way Tomas looked at her.

"Whose child is this?" she asked. I told her Ella was Jesus' child, and He had saved her when she was an infant. As I spoke, she began to cry. You have guessed it by now—it was your own little sparrow, Mia, blown away by the winds but come again in her right mind, and searching for what she had lost.

If you could have seen the joy on her face—and on that of Tomas as well—Millie, you would have known why you had to leave the baby. I wanted you to know that Ella will not be raised by an old bachelor any longer, but by a mommy and a daddy.

I know you have paid a price for your obedience, Charles. But if you could see the church we have built! Good thick adobe walls — with windows donated by my uncle, who attends once a month. The people of Orofino practically raise the rafters when they praise the Lord. Tomas is quite an evangelist. He has started churches in two more villages, and the pastors come here to study the Bible and be trained. Last Sunday Mrs. Quispe came to church with her mouth tight shut and a rag around her head. She had an infected tooth. I thought we might have to get out your old pliers and yank away, but Tupac started to pray for her and God healed her on the spot! She started singing and dancing around, and she has not stopped singing since. I am praying that God will give her the ability to sing on key.

When I sit in the church listening to Tomas preach, I cannot help but wonder what would have happened if Charles and Millie had not come when they were called. I would not have come to the Lord. The church would not have been planted. Little Ella would not have lived.

I am reminded of 1 Peter 1:6–7 when I think of the trials we endured: "In this you greatly rejoice, though now for a little while you may have had to suffer grief in all kinds of trials. These have come so that your faith — of greater worth than gold, which perishes even though refined by fire — may be proved genuine and may result in praise, glory and honor when Jesus Christ is revealed."

The whole church prays for you both, do you know that? It will be a fantastic party when we all meet again in Heaven. Until that time, I remain

> God's missionary
> and your faithful friend,
> Otis

P.S. Send Bibles. We can never have enough. And horehound candy.

Millie found herself crying over Bolivia again, but this time they were tears of joy.

⁓

It was almost a year before Charles was healthy enough to completely take over Dr. Chetwood's practice, and before he did, Millie had news of her own. She whispered it in Charles's ear as they walked home from church. He swallowed and blinked up at the sky. "I hope it's a girl," he said at last.

ear Reader,

God has an adventure planned for you! All life serving Him is an adventure, exciting and full of hope and love. But none of us has a guarantee of how many days we will have on this earth, or the trials or great joys those days will hold.

How will you spend the life you've been given? Will you live a life of faith? Will you serve God where He leads you, even to the ends of the earth? Prayerfully consider making this commitment today:

Lord, I thank You for the life You have given me. I offer it back to You, to use as You wish. I will be Your emissary and Your missionary to the people You love, the ones You died for. Train my mind to resist the devil, and my heart to love the unlovely and the lost. Give me the opportunity and the courage to speak out boldly for You, and to bring many people into Your Kingdom.

If you are not yet a Christian and want to become one, it is as simple as saying a heartfelt prayer, such as the following:

Lord Jesus, I believe that You died on the Cross for our sins and rose from the grave so that we might be forgiven and have eternal life. Please forgive my sins and give me eternal life. Change me to be the person You want me to be, and fulfill the destiny You have planned for me. Amen.

SPECIAL SECTION: A WORLD AT WAR

*T*he world is at war. It is a spiritual battle between God and His enemy, Satan, a fallen angel also known as the devil.

It is important for you to understand that although God and Satan are at war, they are not equals. God is infinite, with no beginning or end. God is omniscient, which means all-knowing; omnipotent, which means all-powerful; and omnipresent, which means everywhere. He is the Creator of the entire universe. Yet He is also our Redeemer and Friend.

Satan, on the other hand, is a created being. He is a powerful angel, but he is *NOT* all-powerful or all-knowing, and he *cannot* be everywhere. He has very limited power and can only operate within parameters that God has allowed.

The Bible refers to Satan as the father of lies, and lying is one of his main weapons against mankind.

∽ IN THE BEGINNING ∽

The spiritual battle against mankind began when Satan, in the form of a serpent, deceived Adam and Eve in the Garden of Eden. Satan lied about several things.

First, he lied about what would happen if they ate from the tree of the knowledge of good and evil in the middle of the garden: "You *will not* surely die," the serpent said to the woman (Genesis 3:4, emphasis added). But God had said, "You are free to eat from any tree in the garden; but you must not eat from the tree of the knowledge of good and evil, for when you eat of it you *will* surely die" (Genesis 2:16-17, emphasis added). Satan tricked Adam and Eve into doubting what God said to them.

Secondly, Satan lied about God's character: "For God *knows* that when you eat of it your eyes will be opened, and you will be like God, knowing good and evil" (Genesis 3:4-5, emphasis added). When Satan said, "For God *knows* that when you eat of it ..." he caused them to doubt God's character. He wanted them to believe that God did not have their best interests in mind, and that God was withholding something good from them. Satan wanted them to think that God did not really love them (which is totally against God's character).

Unfortunately, when Adam and Eve fell for Satan's lies, the world tumbled into darkness.

∞ A DEFEATED FOE ∞

Satan is referred to in the Bible as "the god of this age" (2 Corinthians 4:4). But when Jesus died on the Cross, He defeated Satan and sealed the evil angel's doom forever. God has "rescued us from the dominion of darkness and brought us into the kingdom of the Son he loves, in whom we have redemption, the forgiveness of sins" (Colossians 1:13-14).

Satan's fate is sealed (Revelation 20:10) and he is awaiting his final punishment. But in the meantime, he is full of fury at the knowledge of his defeat. 1 Peter 5:8 tells us that the devil "prowls around like a roaring lion," causing trouble in the world, even for Christians. He fights against the Church, and especially against those who share the Good News of salvation through Jesus Christ.

As an example, the apostle Paul in 1 Thessalonians 2:18 said that he wanted to visit the Thessalonians, but was prevented by Satan. Paul also speaks of "a thorn in my flesh, a messenger of Satan" (2 Corinthians 12:7). Many have speculated that this was an illness, injury, or disability of Paul's. We do not know exactly what this "thorn" was, but we know that Paul pleaded with God three times to remove it. God replied: "My grace is sufficient for you, for my power is made perfect in weakness." God used what Satan meant for evil for good, in order to display His power in Paul's life, and Paul was satisfied to trust in Him, no matter what happened.

✎ PRACTICAL STEPS TO OVERCOME SATAN AND HIS DEMONS ✎

A key to winning your own spiritual battles lies in how you answer the two questions which confronted Adam and Eve, *What did God say?* and *What is God like?*

To answer the first question — *What did God say?* — God has given us the Bible, His Word. When Jesus was tempted in the wilderness, He used Scripture to defeat the lies of Satan. The Truth of God is the best way to silence the evil one. The Bible refers to the Word of God as the *sword* of the Spirit. It is a weapon to combat the enemy! *Stand on what God has said. Read God's Word and, even more importantly, live it!*

To answer the second question — *What is God like?* — God has given us Jesus. Knowing *about* Him is not enough. You must personally and intimately know Him. When you know His feelings, desires, opinions, commands, and promises, you will have a way to protect yourself against deception. *Walk and talk with Jesus, in close fellowship with Him through His Holy Spirit.*

In 2 Corinthians 2, the apostle Paul said, "I have forgiven in the sight of Christ for your sake, in order that Satan might not outwit us. For we are not unaware of his schemes." *Be very aware of how Satan can cause us harm and do not let him outwit you.*

Ephesians 6:18 tells us to "Pray in the Spirit on all occasions with all kinds of prayers and requests. With this in mind, be alert and always keep on praying for all the saints." James 4:7 says, "Resist the devil and he will flee from you." *Resist the enemy's schemes through prayer.*

Ephesians 4 says, "Do not let the sun go down while you are still angry, and do not give the devil a foothold." Things like anger, unforgiveness, bitterness, lying, envy, etc., can make you vulnerable to Satan's attacks. *Do not give the devil an opening through what you do, think, feel, or see.*

While we are to be aware of these things, we must not dwell on the subject of Satan. Our main focus as believers should always be on Jesus Christ. With His life in us, we need not fear!

∽ PROCLAIMING FREEDOM ∽

In Luke 4:18–19, Jesus said:

The Spirit of the Lord is on me,
    because he has anointed me
    to preach good news to the poor.
He has sent me to proclaim freedom for the
    prisoners and recovery of sight for the blind,
    to release the oppressed,
    to proclaim the year of the Lord's favor.

Millie's Fiery Trial

Jesus gives us the great privilege of being His agents to share the message of His love and truth with all those who do not know Him. His offer of forgiveness and salvation is Good News! By spreading this message, we are shattering the darkness, proclaiming freedom, and spreading God's light!

— ABOUT THE AUTHOR —

$\mathcal{M}$artha Finley was born on April 26, 1828, in Chillicothe, Ohio. Her mother died when Martha was quite young, and Dr. James Finley, her father, soon remarried. Martha's stepmother, Mary Finley, was a kind and caring woman who always nurtured Martha's desire to learn and supported her ambition to become a writer.

Dr. Finley was a physician and a devout Christian gentleman. He moved his family to South Bend, Indiana, in the mid-1830s in hopes of a brighter future for his family on the expanding western frontier. Growing up on the frontier as one of eight brothers and sisters surely provided the setting and likely many of the characters for Miss Finley's *Mildred Keith* novels. Considered by many to be partly autobiographical, the books present a fascinating and devoted Christian heroine in the fictional character known as Millie Keith. One can only speculate exactly how much of Martha may have been Millie and vice versa. But regardless, these books nicely complement Miss Finley's bestselling *Elsie Dinsmore* series, which was launched in 1868 and sold millions of copies. The stories of Millie Keith, Elsie's second cousin, were released eight years after the *Elsie* books as a follow-up to that series.

Martha Finley never married and never had children of her own, but she was a remarkable woman who lived a quiet life of creativity and Christian charity. She died at age 81, having written many novels, stories, and books for children and adults. Her life on earth ended in 1909, but her legacy lives on in the wonderful stories of Millie and Elsie.

Collect all of our Millie products

A Life of Faith: Millie Keith Series

* Now Available as a Dramatized Audiobook!

Collect our other
A *Life of Faith* Products!

A Life of Faith: Elsie Dinsmore Series

* Now Available as a Dramatized Audiobook!

Collect all of our Violet products!

A Life of Faith: Violet Travilla Series

Mission City Press

For more information, write to

Mission City Press at 202 Seond Ave. South,
Franklin, Tennessee 37064
or visit our Web Site at:

www.alifeoffaith.com